George Henry Borrow, Ellis Wynne

The Sleeping Bard or Visions of the World, Death, and Hell

George Henry Borrow, Ellis Wynne

The Sleeping Bard or Visions of the World, Death, and Hell

ISBN/EAN: 9783337327040

Printed in Europe, USA, Canada, Australia, Japan

Cover: Foto ©Andreas Hilbeck / pixelio.de

More available books at **www.hansebooks.com**

THE SLEEPING BARD;

OR

Visions of the World, Death, and Hell,

BY

ELIS WYN.

TRANSLATED FROM THE CAMBRIAN BRITISH

BY

GEORGE BORROW,

AUTHOR OF

"THE BIBLE IN SPAIN," "THE GYPSIES OF SPAIN," ETC.

LONDON:
JOHN MURRAY, ALBEMARLE STREET.
1860.

Preface.

The Sleeping Bard was originally written in the Welsh language, and was published about the year 1720. The author of it, Elis Wyn, was a clergyman of the Cambro Anglican Church, and a native of Denbighshire, in which county he passed the greater part of his life, at a place called Y las Ynys. Besides the Sleeping Bard, he wrote and published a book in Welsh, consisting of advice to Christian Professors. The above scanty details comprise all that is known of Elis Wyn. Both his works have enjoyed, and still enjoy, considerable popularity in Wales.

The Sleeping Bard, though a highly remarkable, is not exactly entitled to the appellation of an original work. There are in the Spanish language certain pieces by Francisco Quevedo, called "Visions or Discourses;" the principal ones

being "The Vision of the Carcases, the Sties of Pluto, and
the Inside of the World Disclosed; The Visit of the Gayeties,
and the Intermeddler, the Duenna and the Informer." With
all these the Visions of Elis Wyn have more or less connec-
tion. The idea of the Vision of the World, was clearly
taken from the Interior of the World Disclosed; the idea
of the Vision of Death, from the Vision of the Carcases;
that of the Vision of Hell, from the Sties of Pluto; whilst
many characters and scenes in the three parts, into which
the work of Elis Wyn is divided, are taken either from the
Visit of the Gayeties, the Intermeddler, or others of Quevedo's
Visions; for example Rhywun, or Somebody, who in the
Vision of Death makes the humorous complaint, that so
much of the villainy and scandal of the world is attributed
to him, is neither more nor less than Quevedo's Juan de la
Encina, or Jack o' the Oak, who in the Visit of the Gayeties,
is made to speak somewhat after the following fashion:—

"O ye living people, spawn of Satan that ye are! what is
the reason that ye cannot let me be at rest now that I am dead,
and all is over with me? What have I done to you? What
have I done to cause you to defame me in every thing, who
have a hand in nothing, and to blame me for that of which I
am entirely ignorant?" "Who are you?" said I with a
timorous bow, "for I really do not understand you." "I
am," said he, "the unfortunate Juan de la Encina, whom,

notwithstanding I have been here many years, ye mix up with all the follies which ye do and say during your lives; for all your lives long, whenever you hear of an absurdity, or commit one, you are in the habit of saying, 'Juan de la Encina could not have acted more like a fool;' or, 'that is one of the follies of Juan de la Encina.' I would have you know that all you men, when you say or do foolish things, are Juan de la Encina; for this appellation of Encina, seems wide enough to cover all the absurdities of the world."

Nevertheless, though there is a considerable amount of what is Quevedo's in the Visions of Elis Wyn, there is a vast deal in them which strictly belongs to the Welshman. Upon the whole, the Cambrian work is superior to the Spanish. There is more unity of purpose in it, and it is far less encumbered with useless matter. In reading Quevedo's Visions, it is frequently difficult to guess what the writer is aiming at; not so whilst perusing those of Elis Wyn. It is always clear enough, that the Welshman is either lashing the follies or vices of the world, showing the certainty of death, or endeavouring to keep people from Hell, by conveying to them an idea of the torments to which the guilty are subjected in a future state.

Whether Elis Wyn had ever read the Visions of Quevedo in their original language, it is impossible to say; the probability however is, that he was acquainted with them through the medium of an English translation, which was published in London about the beginning of the eighteenth century; of the merits of that translation the present writer can say nothing, as it has never come to his hand: he cannot however help observing, that a person who would translate the Visions of Quevedo, and certain other writings of his, should be something more than a fair Spanish scholar, and a good master of the language into which he would render them, as they abound not only with idiomatic phrases, but terms of cant or Germanía, which are as unintelligible as Greek or Arabic to the greater part of the Spaniards themselves.

The following translation of the Sleeping Bard has long existed in manuscript. It was made by the writer of these lines in the year 1830, at the request of a little Welsh bookseller of his acquaintance, who resided in the rather unfashionable neighbourhood of Smithfield, and who entertained an opinion that a translation of the work of Elis Wyn, would enjoy a great sale both in England and Wales. On the eve of committing it to the press however, the Cambrian Briton felt his small heart give way within him: "Were I to print it," said he, "I should be ruined; the terrible descriptions of vice and torment, would frighten the genteel part of the English public out of its wits, and I should to a certainty be prosecuted by Sir James Scarlett. I am much obliged to you, for the trouble you have given yourself on my account—but Myn Diawl! I had no idea till I had read him in English, that Elis Wyn had been such a terrible fellow."

Yet there is no harm in the book. It is true that the Author is any thing but mincing in his expressions and descriptions, but there is nothing in the Sleeping Bard which can give offence to any but the over fastidious. There is a great deal of squeamish nonsense in the world; let us hope however that there is not so much as there was. Indeed can we doubt that such folly is on the decline, when we find Albemarle Street in '60, willing to publish a harmless but plain speaking book which Smithfield shrank from in '30?

The Vision of the Course of the World.

One fine evening of warm sunny summer, I took a stroll
to the top of one of the mountains of Wales, carrying with me
a telescope to assist my feeble sight by bringing distant objects
near, and magnifying small ones. Through the thin, clear
air, and the calm and luminous heat, I saw many delightful
prospects afar across the Irish sea. At length, after feasting
my eyes on all the pleasant objects around me, until the sun had
reached his goal in the west, I lay down upon the green grass,
reflecting, how fair and enchanting, from my own country, the
countries appeared whose plains my eyes had glanced over,
how delightful it would be to obtain a full view of them, and
how happy those were who saw the course of the world in
comparison with me: weariness was the result of all this toiling with my eyes and my imagination, and in the shadow of
Weariness, *Mr. Sleep* came stealthily to enthrall me, who
with his keys of lead, locked the windows of my eyes, and
all my other senses securely. But it was in vain for him to

endeavour to lock up the soul, which can live and toil independently of the body, for my spirit escaped out of the locked body upon the wings of Fancy, and the first thing which I saw by the side of me was a dancing ring, and a kind of rabble in green petticoats and red caps dancing away with the most furious eagerness. I stood for a time in perplexity whether I should go to them or not, because in my flurry I feared they were a gang of hungry gipsies, and that they would do nothing less than slaughter me for their supper, and swallow me without salt: but after gazing upon them for some time, I could see that they were better and handsomer than the swarthy, lying Egyptian race. So I ventured to approach them, but very softly, like a hen treading upon hot embers, that I might learn who they were; and at length I took the liberty of addressing them in this guise, with my head and back lowered horizontally: " Fair assembly, as I perceive that you are gentry from distant parts, will you deign to take a Bard along with you, who is desirous of travelling?" At these words the hurly-burly was hushed, and all fixed their eyes upon me: "*Bard*," squeaked one—"*travel*," said another—"*along with us*," said the third. By this time I saw some looking particularly fierce upon me; then they began to whisper in each others ears certain secret words, and to look at me; at length the whispering ceased, and each laying his gripe upon me they raised me upon their shoulders, as we do a knight of the shire, and then away with me they flew like the wind, over houses and fields, cities and kingdoms, seas and mountains; and so quickly did they fly that I could fasten my sight upon nothing, and what was worse, I began to suspect that my companions, by their frowning and knitting their brows at me, wanted me to sing blasphemy against my King and Maker.

"Well," said I to myself, "I may now bid farewell to life, these cursed witches will convey me to the pantry or cellar of some nobleman, and there leave me, to pay with my neck for their robberies; or they will abandon me stark naked, to freeze to death upon the sea-brink of old Shire Caer,* or some other cold, distant place; but on reflecting that all the old hags whom I had once known had long been dead and buried, and perceiving that these people took pleasure in holding or waving me over hollow ravines, I conjectured that they were not witches but beings who are called fairies. We made no stop until I found myself by the side of a huge castle, the most beautiful I had ever seen, with a large pool or moat surrounding it: then they began to consult what they should do with me; "shall we go direct to the castle with him?" said one. "No, let us hang him or cast him into the lake, he is not worth being shown to our great prince," said another. "Did he say his prayers before he went to sleep?" said a third. At the mention of prayers, I uttered a confused groan to heaven for pardon and assistance; and as soon as I recollected myself, I saw a light at a vast distance bursting forth, Oh, how glorious! As it drew nigh, my companions were darkening and vanishing, and quickly there came floating towards us a form of light over the castle, whereupon the fairies abandoned their hold of me, but as they departed they turned upon me a hellish scowl, and unless the angel had supported me, I should have been dashed into pieces small enough for a pasty, by the time I reached the ground.

"What is your business here?" said the angel. "In verity my lord," I replied, "I do not know what place *here* is, nor what is my business, nor what I am myself, nor what has

* Probably Cheshire; the North Welsh commonly call Chester Caer.

become of my other part; I had four limbs and a head, and whether I have left them at home, or whether the fairies, who have certainly not acted fairly with me, have cast me into some abyss, (for I remember to have passed over several horrid ravines,) I cannot tell, sir, though you should cause me to be hung." "Fairly indeed," said he, "they would have acted with you, if I had not come just in time to save you from the clutches of these children of hell."

"Since you have such a particular desire to see the course of the *little world*," said he, "I have received commands to give you a sight of it, in order that you may see your error in being discontented with your station, and your own country. Come with me," he added, "for a peregrination," and at the word he snatched me up, just as the dawn was beginning to break, far above the topmost tower of the castle; we rested in the firmament upon the ledge of a light cloud to gaze upon the rising sun; but my heavenly companion, was far more luminous than the sun, but all his splendour was upward, by reason of a veil which was betwixt him and the nether regions. When the light of the sun became stronger, I could see, between the two luminaries, the vast air-encircled world, like a little round bullet, very far beneath us. "Look now," said the angel, giving me a different telescope from that which I had on the mountain. When I peeped through this I saw things in a manner altogether different from that in which I had seen them before, and in a much clearer one. I saw a city of monstrous size, and thousands of cities and kingdoms within it; and the great ocean, like a moat, around it, and other seas, like rivers, intersecting it.

By dint of long gazing I could see that it was divided into three exceedingly large streets; each street with a large, magnificent gate at the bottom, and each gate with a fair tower over it. Upon each tower there was a damsel of wonderful beauty, standing in the sight of the whole street; and the three towers appeared to reach up behind the walls to the skirts of the castle afore-mentioned. Crossing these three huge streets I could see another; it was but little and mean in comparison with them, but it was clean and neat, and on a higher foundation than the other streets, proceeding upward towards the east, whilst the three others ran downward towards the north to the great gates. I now venturned to enquire of my companion whether I might be permitted to speak. "Certainly," said the angel, "speak out! but listen attentively to my answers, so that I may not have to say the same thing to you more than once." "I will, my lord," said I. "Now pray, what place is the castle yonder in the north?" "The castle above in the air," said he, "belongs to Belial, prince of the power of the air, and governor of all the great city below: it is called Delusive Castle, for Belial is a great deluder, and by his wiles he keeps under his banner all you see, with the exception of the little street yonder. He is a great prince, with thousands of princes under him—what were Cæsar or Alexander the Great compared with him? What are the Turk and old Lewis of France, but his servants? Great, yea, exceeding great, are the power, subtlety, and diligence of the prince Belial; and his armies in the country below are innumerable." "For what purpose," said I, "are the damsels standing yonder, and who are they?" "Softly," said the angel, "one question at once: they are there to be loved and to be adored." "And no wonder indeed," said I, "since they are so amiable; if I possessed feet and hands as formerly, I would go and offer love and adoration to them myself." "Hush,

hush," "said he, "if you would do so with your members, it is well that you are without them; know, thou foolish spirit, that these three princesses are only three destructive deluders, daughters of the prince Belial, and all their beauty and affability, which are irradiating the streets, are only masks over deformity and cruelty; the three within are like their father, replete with deadly poison." "Woe's me; is it possible," said I, quite sad, and smitten with love of them! "It is but too true, alas," said he. "Thou admirest the radiance with which they shine upon their adorers; but know that there is in that radiance a very wondrous charm; it blinds men from looking back, it deafens them lest they should hear their danger, and it burns them with ceaseless longing for more of it: which longing, is itself a deadly poison, breeding, within those who feel it, diseases not to be got rid of, which no physician can cure, not even death, nor anything, unless the heavenly medecine, which is called repentance, is procured, to cast out the evil in time, before it is imbibed too far, by excessive looking upon them." "But how is it," said I, "that Belial does not wish to have these adorers himself?" "He has them," said the angel; "the old fox is adored in his daughters, because, whilst a man sticks to these, or to one of the three, he is securely under the mark of Belial, and wears his livery."

"What are the names," said I, "of those three deceivers?" "The farthest, yonder," said he, "is called *Pride*, the eldest daughter of Belial; the second is *Pleasure*; and *Lucre* is the next to us: these three are the trinity which the world adores." "Pray, has this great, distracted city," said I, "any better name than *Bedlam the Great?*" "It has," he replied, "it is called *The City of Perdition*." "Woe is me," said I, "are all that are contained therein people of perdition?" "The whole," said he, "except some who may escape out to the most high city above, ruled by the king Emmanuel." "Woe's me and mine," said I, "how shall they escape, ever gazing, as they are, upon the thing which blinds them more and more, and which plunders them in their blindness?" "It would be quite impossible," said he, "for one man to escape from thence, did not Emmanuel send his messengers, early and late, from above, to persuade them to turn to him, their lawful King, from the service of the rebel, and also transmit to some, the present of a precious ointment, called *faith*, to anoint their eyes with; and whosoever obtains this *true* ointment, (for there is a counterfeit of it, as there is of every thing else, in the city of Perdition,) and anoints himself with it, will see his wounds, and his madness, and will not tarry a minute longer here, though Belial should give him his three daughters, yea, or the fourth, which is the greatest of all, to do so."

"What are those great streets called?" said I. "Each is called," he replied, "by the name of the princess who governs it: the first is the street of *Pride*, the middle one the street of *Pleasure*, and the nearest, the street of *Lucre*." "Pray tell me," said I, "who are dwelling in these streets? What is the language which they speak? What are the tenets which they hold; and to what nation do they belong?" "Many," said he, "of every language, faith, and nation under the sun, are living in each of those vast streets below; and there are many living in each of the three streets alternately, and every one as near as possible to the gate; and they frequently remove, unable to tarry long in the one, from the great love they bear to the princess of some other street; and the old fox looks slyly on, permitting every one to love his choice, or all three if he pleases, for then he is most sure of him."

"Come nearer to them," said the angel, and hurried with
me downwards, shrouded in his impenetrable veil, through
much noxious vapour which was rising from the city; presently
we descended in the street of Pride, upon a spacious mansion
open at the top, whose windows had been dashed out by dogs
and crows, and whose owners had departed to England or
France, to seek there for what they could have obtained much
easier at home; thus, instead of the good, old, charitable, do-
mestic family of yore, there were none at present but owls,
crows, or chequered magpies, whose hooting, cawing and chattering were excellent comments on the practices of the present
owners. There were in that street, myriads of such abandoned
palaces, which might have been, had it not been for Pride, the
resorts of the best, as of yore, places of refuge for the weak,
schools of peace and of every kind of goodness; and blessings
to thousands of small houses around.

From the summit of this ruin, we had scope and leisure
enough to observe the whole street on either side. There
were fair houses of wondrous height and magnificence—and
no wonder, as there were emperors, kings, and hundreds of
princes there, and thousands of nobles and gentry, and very
many women of every degree. I saw a vain high-topt creature, like a ship at full sail, walking as if in a frame, carrying
about her full the amount of a pedlar's pack, and having at her
ears, the worth of a good farm, in pearls; and there were not
a few of her kind—some were singing, in order that their voices might be praised; some were dancing, to show their figures;
others were painting to improve their complexions; others
had been trimming themselves before the glass, for three hours,
learning to smile, moving pins and making gestures and put-

ting themselves in attitudes. There was many a vain creature there, who did not know how to open her lips to speak, or to eat, nor, from sheer pride, to look under her feet; and many a ragged shrew, who would insist that she was as good a gentlewoman as the best in the street; and many an ambling fop, who could winnow beans with the mere wind of his train.

Whilst I was looking, from afar upon these, and a hundred such, behold! there passed by towards us, a bouncing, variegated lady with a lofty look, and with a hundred folks gazing after her; some bent themselves as if to adore her; some few thrust something into her hand. Being unable to imagine who she was, I enquired. "Oh," replied my friend, "she is one who has all her portion in sight, yet you see how many foolish people are seeking her, and the meanest of them in possession of all the attainments she can boast of. *She will not have what she can gain, and will never gain what she desires*, and she will speak to no one but her betters, on account of her mother's telling her, 'that a young woman cannot do a worse thing, than be humble in her love.'" Thereupon came out from beneath us a pillar of a man, who had been an alderman, and in many official situations; he came spreading his wings as if to fly, though he could scarcely draw one knee after the other, on account of the gout, and various other genteel disorders: notwithstanding which, you could not obtain from him, but through a very great favour, a glance or a nod, though you should call him by his titles and his offices.

From this being I turned my eyes to the other side of the street, where I beheld a lusty young nobleman, with a number of people behind him; he had a sweet smile and a condescending air to every one who met him. "It is strange," said I, "that this young man and yonder personage should belong to the same street." " Oh, the same princess Pride rules them both," answered the angel,—" this young man is only speaking fair on account of the errand he comes upon; he is seeking popularity at present, with the intent to raise himself thereby to the highest office in the kingdom— it is easy for him to lament to the people how much they are wronged by the oppression of bad masters; but his own ex- altment, and not the weal of the kingdom, is the heart of the matter." After gazing for a long time, I perceived at the gate of Pride, a fair city upon seven hills, and on the top of its lofty palace there was a triple crown, with swords and keys crossed. " Lo! there is Rome," said I, " and therein dwells the Pope." " Yes, most usually," said the angel; " but he has a palace in each of the other streets." Over against Rome, I could see a city with an exceedingly fair palace, and upon it was mounted on high, a half-moon on a banner of gold, and by that I knew that the Turk was there. Next to the gate after those, was the palace of Lewis xiv., of France, as I un- derstood by his arms, three fleurs-de-lis upon a silver banner hanging aloft. Whilst looking on the height and majesty of these palaces, I perceived that there was much passing and repassing from the one to the other, and I asked what was the cause thereof? " Oh, there is many a dark cause," said the angel, " why those three crafty, powerful heads should communicate; but though they account themselves fully adapted to espouse the three princesses above, their power and subtlety are nothing when compared with these; yes, Belial the Great does not esteem the whole city, (though so numerous be its kings), as equivalent to his daughters. Not- withstanding that he offers them in marriage to everybody, he has still never given one entirely to anybody yet. There has been a rivalry between these three concerning them:—the Turk, who calls himself *God upon earth*, wished for the eldest, Pride, in marriage. 'No,' said the king of France, 'she belongs to me, as I keep all my subjects in her street, and likewise bring many to her from England and other countries.' Spain would have the princess Lucre, in despite of Holland and all the Jews. England would have the princess Pleasure, in despite of the Pagans. But the Pope would have the whole three, and with better reason than all the rest together, therefore Belial has stationed him next to them in the three streets." "And is it on this account that there is this intercourse at present," said I. "No;" he replied, " Belial has arranged the matter between them for some time; but at present he has caused them to lay their heads together, how they may best destroy the cross street yonder, which is the city of Emmanuel, and particularly one great palace which is there, out of sheer venom at perceiving that it is a fairer edifice than exists in all the city of Perdition. Belial moreover has promised to those who shall accomplish its destruction, the half of his kingdom during his life, and the whole when he is dead. But, notwithstanding the greatness of his power and the depth of his wiles; notwithstanding the multitude of crafty emperors, kings, and rulers, who are beneath his banner in the vast city of Perdition; and notwithstanding the bravery of his countless legions on the outer side of the gates in the world below; notwithstanding all this," said the angel, " he shall see that it is a task above his power to perform. Yes; however great Belial may be, he shall find that there is One greater than he, in the little street yonder."

I was unable to hear his angelic reasons completely, from the tumbling there was along this slippery street every hour,

and I could see some people with ladders scaling the tower,
and having reached the highest step fall headlong to the
bottom. "To what place are those fools seeking to get?"
said I. "To a place high enough," said he; "they are seeking to break into the treasury of the princess." "I will
warrant it is full enough," said I. "It is," he replied; "and
with every thing which belongs to this street, for the purpose
of being distributed amongst the inhabitants. There you will
find every species of warlike arms to subdue and to over-run
countries; every species of arms of gentility, banners, escutche-
ons, books of pedigree, stanzas and poems relating to ancestry,
with every species of brave garments; admirable stories, lying
portraits; all kinds of tints and waters to embellish the countenance; all sorts of high offices and titles; and, to be brief,
there is every thing there that is adapted to cause a man to
think better of himself, and worse of others than he ought.
The chief officers of this treasury are masters of ceremonies,
vagabonds, genealogists, bards, orators, flatterers, dancers,
tailors, mantua-makers, and the like." From this great
street we proceeded to the next, where the princess Lucre
reigns; it was a full and prodigiously wealthy street, yet
not half so splendid and clean as the street of Pride, nor its
people half so bold and lofty looking: for they were skulking
mean-looking fellows, for the most part.

There were in this street thousands of Spainards, Hol-
landers, Venetians, and Jews, and a great many aged,
decrepit people were also there. "Pray, sir," said I, "what
kind of men are these?" "They have all gain in view," said
he. "At the lowest extremity, on one side, you will still see
the Pope; also subduers of kingdoms and their soldiers, op-
pressors, foresters, shutters up of the common foot-paths.

justices and their bribers, and the whole race of lawyers down
to the catchpole. On the other side," said he, "there are
physicians, apothecaries, doctors, misers, merchants, extortioners, usurers, refusers to pay tithes, wages, rents, or alms
which were left to schools and charity houses; purveyors
and chapmen who keep and raise the market to their own
price; shopkeepers (or sharpers) who make money out of
the necessity or ignorance of the buyer; stewards of every
degree, sturdy beggars, taverners who plunder the families of
careless men of their property, and the country of its barley
for the bread of the poor. All these are thieves of the first
water," said he; "and the rest are petty thieves, for the most
part, and keep at the upper end of the street; they consist of
high-way robbers, tailors, weavers, millers, measurers of wet
and dry, and the like." In the midst of this discourse, I heard a
prodigious tumult at the lower end of the street, where there
was a huge crowd of people thronging towards the gate, with
such pushing and disputing as caused me to imagine that
there was a general fray on foot, until I demanded of my
friend what was the matter. "There is an exceeding great
treasure in that tower," said the angel, "and all that concourse is for the purpose of choosing a treasurer to the princess, in lieu of the Pope, who has been turned out of that
office." So we went to see the election.

The men who were competing for the office were the
Stewards, the *Usurers,* the *Lawyers,* and the *Merchants,* and
the richest of the whole was to obtain it, because the more
you have the more you shall crave, is the epidemic curse of
the street. The Stewards were rejected at the first offer, lest
they should impoverish the whole street, and, as they had
raised their palaces on the ruins of their masters, lest they

should in the end turn the princess out of her possession; then the dispute arose between the three others; the Merchants had the most silks, the Lawyers most mortgages on lands, and the Usurers the greatest number of full bags, and bills and bonds. "Ha! they will not agree to night," said the angel, so come away; "the Lawyers are richer than the Merchants, the Usurers are richer than the Lawyers, and the Stewards than the Usurers, and Belial than the whole, for he owns them all, and their property too."

"For what reason is the princess keeping these thieves about her?" I demanded. "What can be more proper," said he, "when she herself is the arrantest of thieves." I was astonished to hear him call the princess thus, and the greatest potentates thieves of the first water." "Pray, my lord," said I, "how can you call those illustrious people greater thieves than robbers on the highway?" "You are but a dupe," said he; "is not the villain who goes over the world with his sword in his hand and his plunderers behind him, burning and slaying, wresting kingdoms from their right owners, and looking forward to be adored as a conqueror, worse than the rogue who takes a purse upon the highway? What is the tailor who cabbages a piece of cloth, to the great man who takes a piece out of the parish common? Ought not the latter to be called a thief of the first water, or ten times more a rogue than the other?— the tailor merely takes snips of cloth from his customer, whilst the other takes from the poor man the sustenance of his beast, and by so doing the sustenance of himself and his little ones—what is taking a handful of flour at the mill, to keeping a hundred sacksfull to putrify, in order to obtain afterwards a four-fold price?—what is the half-naked soldier who takes your garment away with his sword, to the lawyer, who takes your whole estate from you with a goose's quill, without any claim or bond upon it?—and what is the pickpocket who takes five pounds, to the cogger of dice who will cheat you of a hundred in the third part of a night?—and what is the jockey who tricks you in some old unsound horse, to the apothecary who chouses you of your money, and your life also with some old unwholesome physic?—and yet what are all these thieves to the mistress-thief there, who takes away from the whole all these things, and their hearts and their souls at the end of the fair?" From this dirty, disorderly street we proceeded to the street of the princess Pleasure, in which I beheld a number of Britons, French, Italians, Pagans, &c. She was a princess exceedingly beautiful to the eye, with a cup of drugged wine in the one hand, and a crown and a harp in the other. In her treasury there were numberless pleasures and pretty things to obtain the custom of every body, and to keep them in the service of her father. Yea! there were many who escaped to this charming street, to cast off the melancholy arising from their losses and debts in the other streets. It was a street prodigiously crowded, especially with young people; and the princess was careful to please every body, and to keep an arrow adapted to every mark. If you are thirsty, you can have here your choice of drink; if you love dancing and singing, you can get here your fill. If her comeliness entice you to lust for the body of a female, she has only to lift up her finger to one of the officers of her father, (who surround her at all times, though invisibly), and they will fetch you a lass in a minute, or the *body* of a harlot newly buried, and will go into her in lieu of a *soul*, rather than you should abandon so good a design.

Here there are handsome houses with very pleasant gardens, teeming orchards, and shadowy groves, adapted to all kinds of secret meetings, in which one can hunt birds and a certain fair coney; here there are delightful rivers for fishing, and wide fields hedged around, in which it is pleasant to hunt the hare and fox. All along the street you could see farces being acted, juggling going on, and all kinds of tricks of legerdemain; there was plenty of licentious music, vocal and instrumental, ballad singing, and every species of merriment; there was no lack of male and female beauty, singing and dancing; and there were here many from the street of Pride, who came to receive praise and adoration. In the interior of the houses I could see people on beds of silk and down, wallowing in voluptuousness; some were engaged at billiard-playing, and were occasionally swearing or cursing the table keeper; others were rattling the dice or shuffling the cards. My guide pointed out to me some from the street of Lucre, who had chambers in this street; they had run hither to reckon their money, but they did not tarry long lest some of the innumerable tempting things to be met with here should induce them to part with their pelf, without usury. I could see throngs of individuals feasting, with something of every creature before them; oh, how every one did gorge, swallowing mess after mess of dainties, sufficient to have feasted a moderate man for three weeks, and when they could eat no more, they belched out a thanks for what they had received, and then gave the health of the king and every jolly companion; after which, they drowned the savour of the food, and their cares besides, in an ocean of wine; then they called for tobacco, and began telling stories of their neighbours—and, I observed, that all the stories were well received, whether true

or false, provided they were amusing and of late date, above
all if they contained plenty of scandal: there they sat, each
with his clay pistol puffing forth fire and smoke, and slander
to his neighbour. At length I was fain to request my guide
to permit me to move on; the floor was impure with saliva
and spilt drink, and I was apprehensive that certain heavy
hiccups which I heard, might be merely the prelude to something more disagreeable.

From thence we went to a place where we heard a terrible
noise, a medley of striking, jabbering, crying and laughing,
shouting and singing. "Here's Bedlam, doubtless," said I.
By the time we entered the den the brawling had ceased.
Of the company, one was on the ground insensible; another
was in a yet more deplorable condition; another was nodding
over a hearthful of battered pots, pieces of pipes, and oozings
of ale. And what was all this, upon enquiry, but a carousal
of seven thirsty neighbours—a goldsmith, a pilot, a smith,
a miner, a chimney-sweeper, a poet, and a parson who had
come to preach sobriety, and to exhibit in himself what a
disgusting thing drunkenness is. The origin of the last
squabble was a dispute which had arisen among them, about
which of the seven loved a pipe and flagon best. The poet
had carried the day over all the rest, with the exception of
the parson, who, out of respect for his cloth, had the most
votes, being placed at the head of the jolly companions—the
poet singing:—

> "Oh, where are there seven beneath the sky,
> Who with these seven for thirst can vie ?
> But the best for good ale, these seven among,
> Are the jolly divine, and the son of song."

Disgusted with these drunken swine, we went nearer to

the gate, to take a peep at the follies of the palace of *Love*,
the purblind king; it is a place easy to enter and difficult to
escape from, and in it there is a prodigious number of chambers.   In the hall opposite to the door was insane Cupid,
with his two arrows upon his bow, shooting tormenting
poison, which is called *bliss*.   Upon the floor I could see
many fair damsels, finely dressed, walking about, and behind
them a parcel of miserable youths gazing upon their beauty,
and each eager to obtain a glance from his mistress, fearing
her frown far worse than death.   One was bending to the
ground and placing a letter in the hands of his goddess;
another a piece of music, all in fearful expectation, like school-
boys showing their tasks to their master; and the damsels
would glance back upon them a smile, to keep up the fervour
of their adorers, but nothing more, lest they should lose their
desire, become cured of their wound and depart.   On going
forward to the parlour, I beheld females learning to dance and
to sing, and to play on instruments, for the purpose of making
their lovers seven times more foolish than they were already:
on going to the buttery, I found them taking lessons in deli-
cacy and propriety of eating: on going to the cellar, I saw them
making up potent love drinks, from nail-parings and the like:
on going to the chambers, we beheld a fellow in a secret apart-
ment, putting himself into all kinds of attitudes, to teach his
beloved elegant manners; another learning in a glass to laugh
in a becoming manner, without showing to his love too much
of his teeth; another we found embellishing his tale before
going to her, and repeating the same lesson a hundred times.
Tired of this insiped folly, I went to another chamber, where
there was a nobleman, who had sent for a bard from the street
of Pride, to compose a eulogistic strain on his angel, and a

laudatory ode on himself: the bard was haranguing upon his talent—"I can," said he, "compare her to all the red and white under the sun, and say that her hair is a hundredfold more yellow than gold; and as for your ode, I can carry your genealogy through the bowels of an infinity of knights and princes, and through the waters of the deluge, even as high up as Adam." "Lo!" said I, "here is a bard who is a better inventor than myself." "Come away, come away," said the angel, "these people are thinking to bamboozle the woman, but when they go to her, they will be sure to obtain from her as good as they bring."

On leaving these people, we caught a glimpse of some cells, where more obscene practices were going on, than modesty will suffer me to mention, which caused my companion to snatch me away in wrath, from this palace of whimsicality and wantonness, to the treasury of the princess, (because we went where we pleased, in spite of doors and locks.) There we beheld a multitude of beautiful damsels, all sorts of drink, fruit, and dainties; all kinds of instruments and books of music, harps, pipes, poems, carols, &c.; all kinds of games of chance, draught-boards, dice-boxes, dice, cards, &c.; all kinds of models of banquets and mansions, figures of men, contrivances and amusements: all kinds of waters, perfumes, colors and salves to make the ugly handsome, and the old look young, and to make the harlot and her putrid bones sweet for a time.

To be brief, there were here all kinds of *shadows* of pleasure, all kinds of *seeming* delight; and to tell the truth, I believe this place would have ensnared me, had not my friend, without ceremony, snatched me far away from the three deceitful towers, to the upper end of the street, and set me down by a castellated palace of prodigious size, and very agreeable

at first sight, but vile and terribly revolting on the farthest
side, though it was only seen with great difficulty on the side of
its deformity; it had a multitude of doors, and all the doors
were splendid on the outside, but filthy within. "Pray, my
lord," said I. "if it please you, what is this wonderful place?"
"This," said he, "is the palace of another daughter of Belial,
who is called *Hypocrisy;* she here keeps her school; there
is not a youth or damsel within the whole city, that has not
been her scholar, and the people in general, have so well imbibed what she has taught, that her lessons have become a
second nature, and intertwined with all their thoughts, words
and actions, almost since the time of their childhood. After I
had inspected for a time the falsehood of every corner of the
edifice, a procession passed by with a deal of weeping and
groaning, and many men and horses dight in habits of deep
mourning. Presently came a wretched widow, closely muffled,
in order that she might look no more on this vile world; she
was feebly crying, and groaning slowly in the intervals of
fainting fits—verily, I could not help weeping myself, out of
pity. "Pooh, pooh," said the angel, "keep your tears for
something more worthy; these faintings are only a lesson of
Hypocrisy, and in her great school these black garments were
fashioned. There is not one of these people weeping seriously;
the widow, before the body left the house, had wedded another
man, in her heart; and if she could get rid of the expense
attending the body, she would not care a rush if the soul of her
husband were at the bottom of hell; nor would her relations,
more than herself; because when his disease was hardest upon
him, instead of giving him salutary counsel and praying fer-
vently, for the Lord to have mercy upon him, they only talked
to him about his effects, and about his testament, or his pedi-

gree, or what a handsome vigorous man he had been, and the like; so all this lamenting is mere sham—some are mourning in obedience to custom and habit, others for company's sake, and others for hire.

Scarcely had this procession passed by, when, lo, another crowd came in sight. A certain nobleman, prodigiously magnificient, and his lady at his side, were going along in state; many respectable men were capping them, and there were a thousand also behind them, shewing them every kind of submission and reverence, and by the *favours*, I perceived that it was a wedding: "He must be a very exalted nobleman," said I, "who merits so much respect from all these people. "If you should consider the whole, you would say something quite different," said my guide: "that nobleman is one from the street of Pleasure; and the female, is a damsel from the street of Pride, and the old man yonder, who is speaking with him, is one from the street of Lucre, who has lent money upon nearly all the land of the nobleman, and is to-day come to settle accounts. We drew nigh to hear the conversation.

"Verily, sir," says the usurer, "I would not for all I possess, that you should want any thing that I can offer, in order that you may appear to-day like yourself, especially since you have met with a lady so amiable and illustrious as this." (The subtle old dog knowing perfectly well what she was all the time.) "By the Lord above," said the nobleman, "the next greatest pleasure, to looking at her beauty, is to listen to your obliging discourse; I would rather pay you usury than obtain money gratis from any one else." "Of a surety, my lord," said one of his principal associates, who was called flatterer, "my uncle shows you no respect but what is fully your right; but with your permission, I will assert, that he has not bestowed half the commendation on her ladyship which she deserves. I cannot myself produce, and I will defy any man to produce one lovelier than herself, in the whole street of Pride; nor one more gallant than you, my lord, in the whole street of Pleasure; nor one more courteous than you, dear uncle, in the whole street of Lucre." "Oh, that is only your good opinion," replied the lord, "but I certainly believe that two never came together with more mutual love than we." As they proceeded, the crowd increased, and every one had a fair smile and a low bow for the other, and forward they ran to meet each other with their noses to the ground, like two cocks going to engage. "Know now," said the angel, "that you have not yet seen a *bow* here, nor heard a *word*, that did not belong to the lessons of Hypocrisy. There is not here one, after all this courtesy, that has a farthing's worth of love for the other; indeed they are for the most part enemies to one another. The nobleman here is only a butt amongst them, and every one has his hit at him. The lady has her mind fixed upon his *grandeur* and his *nobility*, whereby she hopes to obtain precedence over many of her acquaintances. The miser has his eye upon his *land*, for his own son: and the others, to a man, on the money, which he is to receive as her portion, because they are all his subjects, that is, his merchants, his tailors, his shoemakers, or his other tradesmen, who have arrayed him and maintained him in all this great splendour, without yet obtaining one farthing, nor any thing but fair words, and now and then, threats perhaps. Now observe how many masks, how many twists, Hypocrisy has given to the face of the truth? He is promising grandeur to his love, having already disposed of his land; and she is promising portion and purity, whereas she has no purity, but purity of dress, and as for her portion it will not be long in existence, there being an inveterate cancer in it, even as there is in her own body."

"Well, here is a proof," said I, "that one never ought to judge by appearances." "Yes," said he, "but come away, and I will show you something more." Whereupon he transported me up to where stood the churches of the city of Perdition, for every body in it had an appearance of faith, even in the age of Disbelief. First we went to the temple of Heathenism, where I could see some adoring the form of a man, others that of the sun, others that of the moon, and an innumerable quantity of similar other gods, even down to leek and garlick, and a great goddess termed *Delusion*, obtaining general adoration, although you might see something of the remnants of the Christian faith amongst some of these people. Thence we went to a meeting of Dummies, where there was nothing but groaning, and shivering, and beating the breast. "Though there is here," said the angel, " an appearance of repentance and great submission, there is nothing in reality, but opinionativeness and obstinacy, and pride, and thick, thick darkness. Notwithstanding they talk so much about their *internal light*, they have not even the spectacle-glasses of nature which the heathens have, whom you lately saw." From these dumb dogs we chanced to turn to a large church open at the top, with a prodigious number of sandals† at the gate, by which I knew that it was the temple of the Turks; these people had only a dim and motley colored spectacle glass, which they called the Koran, yet through this they were always gazing up to the top of the church for their prophet, who, according to the promise

† It is the custom of Mahometans, to lay aside their sandals, before entering the Mosque.

which he gave them, ought to have returned to them long ago, but has not yet made his appearance. From there we went to the church of the Jews, people who had failed to find the way of escape from the city of Perdition, although they possessed a pure, clear spectacle glass, on account of a film having come over their eyes from long gazing, for want of having anointed them with the precious ointment, *faith*. We next went to that of the Papists. "Behold," said the angel, "the church which *deceiveth the nations!* Hypocrisy has built this church at her own expense; for the Papists permit, yea, enjoin the breaking of any oath made to a heretic, although it were taken upon the sacrament." From the chancel we passed through key-holes to the upper end of a cell which stood apart, full of burning candles at mid-day, where we perceived a priest with his crown shaven, walking about as if he were in expectation of visitors; presently there came a rotund figure of a woman, and a very pretty girl behind her, and they went upon their knees before him to confess their sins. "My spiritual father," said the good woman, "I labour under a burden too heavy to be borne, unless you in your mercy will lighten it; I married a member of the church of England, and"—"What," said the shaven crown, "married a heretic! married an enemy! there is no pardon for you, now or ever." At this word she fainted, and he vociferated curses at her. "Oh, and what is worse," said she when she revived, "I have killed him!" "O, ho! you have killed him, well that is something towards obtaining reconciliation with the church; but I assure you, that unless you had killed him, you would never have got absolution, nor purgatory, but would have gone plump to the devil. But where is your offering to the cloister?" said he, snarling. "Here," she replied, and handed him a pretty big purse of money. "Well," said he, "I will now make your peace, and your penance is to remain a widow as long as you live, lest you should make another bad bargain." As soon as she had departed, the damsel came forward to make her confession. " Your pardon, my father confessor," said she, "I have borne a child and murdered it." "Very fair, in troth," said the confessor, "and who was the father?" "Verily," said she, "it was one of your monastery" —"Hush, hush," said he, "no scandal against the men of the church: but where is your atonement to the church?" "There," said she, handing him a gold coin. "You must repent, and your penance is to watch to night by my bedside," said he, smiling archly upon her.

At this moment appeared four other bald-pates, hauling in a lad to the confessor, the poor fellow looking as pleased as if he were going to the gallows. "We have brought you a cub," said one of the four, "that you may award him a proper punishment for revealing the secrets of the catholic church." "What secrets?" said the confessor, looking towards a murky cell which was nigh at hand. "But confess villain, what did you say?" "In truth," said the wretch, "one of my acquaintances asked me, if I had seen the *souls* shrieking beneath the altar, *on the day of the festival of the dead?* And I said, that I had heard the voice, but that I had seen nothing." "Ah, sir, say the whole," said one of the others. "But I added," said he, "that I had heard that you were only deceiving us ignorant people, and that instead of souls shrieking, there were only sea-crabs crackling beneath the carpet," —"O son of the fiend! blasphemous monster!" said the confessor; "but proceed caitiff."—"and that it was a wire which turned the image of saint Peter," said the fellow, "and

that it was by the wire that the Holy Ghost descended from
the gallery of the cross upon the priest." "O heritage of hell!"
said the confessor. "Soho here! take him torturers, and cast
him into the smoky chimney yonder for telling tales." "Here
you see," said the angel, "the church which Hypocrisy desires
should be called the Catholic Church, and the members of
which she would fain have the world consider, as the only
people destined to be saved; it must be owned, indeed, that
they had the true spectacle-glass, but they spoiled it by cut-
ting upon the glass numerous images; and they had true faith,
but they mingled that precious ointment with their own novel
inventions, so that at present they see no more than the
heathen." Thence we went to a barn, where stood a pert,
conceited fellow preaching with great glibness, frequently
repeating the same thing three times. "This man and his
hearers," said the angel, "possess the true spectacle-glass, to
see the things which pertain to their peace, but they lack now
in their old age, a very essential matter which is called perfect
love. Various are the causes which drive folks hither; some
come out of respect to their forefathers, some out of ignorance,
and many for worldly advantage. They will make you believe
with their faces that they are being strangled, but they can
swallow a toad if necessary; and thus the princess Hypocrisy
does not disdain to teach some in barns." "Pray," said I,
"where now is the *Church of England?*" "O," said he, "in
the city high above, it constitutes a great part of the *Catholic
Church,* and in the city here below, there are some probation-
ary churches belonging to it, where the English and Welsh
are under probation for a time, in order to become qualified
to have their names written in the book of the Catholic
Church, and they who become so, *blessed are they for ever.* But

alas, there are but very few who are adapting themselves to obtain honour above; because, instead of looking thitherward, too many suffer themselves to be blinded by the three princesses below, and Hypocrisy keeps many with one eye upon the city above, and the other on that below; yea, Hypocrisy has succeeded in enticing many from their path, after they have overcome the three other deceivers. Come in here," said he, "and you will see something more;" whereupon he carried me to the gallery of one of the churches in Wales, the people being in the midst of the service. And lo! some were whispering, talking and laughing; some looking upon the pretty women; others were examining the dress of their neighbours from top to toe; some were pushing themselves forward and snarling at one another about rank; some were dozing; others were busily engaged in their devotions, but many of these were playing a hypocritical part "You have not seen yet," said the angel, "no, not amongst the infidels, shamelessness as open and barefaced as this: but thus, alas, we see *that the corruption of the best thing is the corruption worst of all.*" The congregation then proceeded to take the sacrament, and every one displayed reverential feelings at the altar.

However, (through the glass of my companion,) I could see one receiving the bread into his belly, under the figure of a *mastiff*, another under that of a *swine*, another like a *mole*, another like a *winged serpent*, and a few, O how very few, receiving a ray of celestial light with the bread and the wine. "Yonder," said he, "is a roundhead who is about to become sheriff, and because the law enjoins, that every one shall receive the communion in the church before he obtains the office, he has come hither rather than lose it; but though there are many here who rejoice at seeing him, there has been no joy amongst us for his conversion, for he has only turned for the time; and thus you see how bold Hypocrisy must be to present herself at the altar before Emmanuel, who is not to be deceived. But however great she be in the city of Perdition, she can effect nothing in the city of Emmanuel, above the wall yonder."

Thereupon we turned our faces from the great city of Perdition, and went up to the other little city. In going along I could see at the upper end of the streets, many turning half-way from the temptations of the *gates of Perdition*, and seeking for the *gate of Life;* but whether it was that they failed to find it, or grew tired upon the way, I could not see that any went through, except one sorrowful faced man, who ran forward resolutely, while thousands on each side of him were calling him fool, some scoffing him, others threatening him, and his friends laying hold upon him, and entreating him not to take a step by which he would lose the whole world at once. "I only lose," said he, "a very small portion of it, and if I should lose the whole, pray what loss is it? For what is there in the world so desirable, unless a man should desire deceit, and violence, and misery, and wretchedness, giddiness and distraction. *Contentment and tranquillity*," said he, "constitute the happiness of man; but in your city there are no such things to be found. Because who is there here content with his station? *Higher, higher*, is what every one endeavours to be in the street of *Pride;* give, give us a little more, says every one in the street of *Lucre;* sweet, sweet, pray give me some more of it, is the cry of every one in the street of *Pleasure.* And as for tranquillity, where is it? and who obtains it? If you be a great man, flattery and envy are killing you; if you be poor, every one is trampling upon and despi-

sing you; after having become an inventor, if you exalt your
head and seek for praise, you will be called a boaster and a
coxcomb; if you lead a godly life and resort to the church
and the altar, you will be called a hypocrite; if you do not,
then you are an infidel or a heretic; if you be merry, you will
be called a buffoon; if you are silent, you will be called a
morose wretch; if you follow honesty, you are nothing but a
simple fool; if you go neat, you are proud, if not, a swine; if
you are smooth speaking, then you are false, or a trifler
without meaning; if you are rough, you are an arrogant,
disagreeable devil. Behold the world that you magnify,"
said he, "pray take my share of it." Whereupon he shook
himself loose from them all, and away he went undauntedly to
the narrow gate, and in spite of every obstacle he pushed his
way through, we following him; while many men dressed in
black upon the walls, on both sides of the gate, kept inviting
the man and praising him. "Who," said I, "are the men above
dressed in black?" "The watchmen of the king Emmanuel,"
replied the angel, "who, in the name of their master, are
inviting people and assisting them through this gate."

By this time we were by the gate; it was very low and
narrow, and mean in comparison with the lower gates. On the
two sides of the door were the *ten commandments;* upon the
first slab on the right side was written, "*love the Lord with thy
whole heart, &c.,*" and upon the second slab on the other side,
"*love thy neighbour as thyself;*" and above the whole, "*love
not the world nor the things which are therein.*" I had not
looked long before the watchmen began to cry out to the men
of Perdition, "Flee! flee, for your lives!" Only a very few
turned towards them once, some of whom asked, "flee from
what?" "From the prince of this world, who reigns in the

children of disobedience," said the watchman; "flee from the
pollutions which are in the world through the lusts of the
flesh, the lusts of the eyes, and the vanities of life; flee from
the wrath which is coming to overwhelm you!" "What,"
exclaimed the other watchman, "is your beloved city, but a
vast glowing roof cast over Hell, and if you were here, you
might see the fire on the farther side of your walls kindling,
to burn you down into Hell." Some mocked them, others
threatened to stone them unless they ceased their unmannerly
prate; but some few asked, "whither shall we fly?" "Hither,"
said the watchman, "fly hither to your lawful king, who yet
offers you pardon through us, if you return to your obedience,
and abandon the rebel Belial and his deceitful daughters.
Though their appearance is so splendid, it is only deception;
Belial at home is but a very poor prince, he has only you for
fuel, and only you as roast and boiled to gnaw, and you are
never sufficient, and there will never be an end to his hunger
and your torments. And who would serve such a malicious
butcher, in a temporary delirium here, and in eternal torments
hereafter, who could obtain a life of happiness under a king
merciful and charitable to his subjects, who is ever doing
towards them the good offices of a shepherd, and endeavouring
to keep them from Belial, in order finally to give to each of
them the kingdom in the country of Light? O fools! will ye
take the horrible enemy whose throat is burning with thirst
for your blood, instead of the compassionate prince who has
given his own blood to assist you?" But it did not appear
that these reasonings, which were sufficient to soften a rock,
proved of much advantage to them, and the principal cause
of their being so unsuccessful was, that not many had leisure
to hear, the greater part being employed in looking at the

gates; and of those who did hear, there were not many who heeded, and of those there were not many who long remembered; some would not believe that it was Belial whom they were serving, others could not conceive that yonder little, untrodden passage was the gate of Life, and would not believe that the three other glittering gates were delusion, the castle preventing them from seeing their destruction till they rushed upon it.

At this moment there came a troop of people from the street of Pride, and knocked at the gate with great confidence but they were all so stiffnecked, that they could never go into a place so low, without soiling their perriwigs and their plumes, so they walked back in great ill humour. At the tail of these came a party from the street of Lucre. Said one, "is this the gate of Life?" "Yea," replied the watchmen who were above. "What is to be done," said he, "in order to pass through?" "Read on each side of the door, and you will learn." The miser read the ten commandments. "Who," he cried, "will say, that I have broken one of these?" But on looking aloft and seeing, "*love not the world, nor the things that are therein*," he started, and could not swallow that difficult sentence. There was among them an envious pig-tail who turned back on reading, "*love thy neighbour as thyself*;" and a perjurer, and a slanderer turned abruptly back on reading, "*bear not false witness*;" some physicians on reading, "*thou shalt commit no murder*," exclaimed "this is no place for us." To be brief, every one saw there something which troubled him, so they all went back to chew the end. I may add, that there was not one of these people, but had so many bags and writings stuck about him, that he could never have gone through a place so narrow, even if he had made the attempt.

Presently there came a drove from the street of Pleasure walking towards the gate. "Please to inform us," said one to the watchmen, "to what place this road is leading?" This is the road," said the watchman, "which leads to eternal joy and happiness;" whereupon they all strove to get through, but they failed, for some had too much belly for a place so narrow; others were too weak to push, having been enfeebled by women, who impeded them moreover with their foolish whims. "O," said the watchman who was looking upon them, "it is of no use for you to attempt to go through with your vain toys; you must leave your pots, and your dishes, and your harlots, and all your other ware behind you, and then make haste." "How should we live then?" said the fiddler, who would have been through long ago, but for fear of breaking his instrument. "O," said the watchman, "you must take the word of the king, for sending you whatsover things may be for your advantage." "Hey, hey," said one, "*a bird in the hand is worth two in the bush*;" and thereupon they all unanimously turned back.

"Come through now," said the angel, and he drew me in, and the first thing I saw in the porch was a large baptismal font, and by the side of it a spring of saline water. "Why is this here at the entrance of the road?" said I. "It is here," said the angel, "because every one must wash himself therein, previous to obtaining honour in the palace of Emmanuel; it is termed the *fountain of repentance*." Above I could see written, "*this is the gate of the Lord, &c.*" The porch and also the street expanded, and became less difficult as one went forward. When we had gone a little way up the street, I could hear a soft voice behind me saying, "*this is the road, walk in it.*" The street was up-hill but was very clean and straight, and though the houses were lower here than in the city of *Perdition*, yet they were more pleasant. If there is here less wealth. there is also less strife and care; if there are fewer dishes, there are fewer diseases; if there is less noise, there is also less sadness, and more pure joy. I was surprised at the calmness and the delightful tranquillity that reigned here, so little resembling what I had found below. Instead of swearing and cursing, buffoonery, debauchery, and drunkenness; instead of pride and vanity, torpor in the one corner, and riot in the other; instead of all the loud broiling, and the boasting, and bustling, and chattering, which were incessantly stupifying a man yonder; and instead of the numberless constant evils to be found below, you here saw sobriety, affability and cheerfulness, peace and thankfulness, clemency, innocence, and content upon the face of every body. No weeping here, except for the pollutions pervading the city of the enemy; no hatred or anger, except against sin; and that same hatred and anger against sin, always accompanied with a certainty of being able to subdue it: no fear but of incensing the King, who was ever more ready to forgive than be angry with his subjects; and here there was no sound but of psalms of praise to the heavenly guardian.

By this time we had come in sight of a building superlatively beautiful. O, how glorious it was! No one in the city of Perdition—neither the Turk nor the Mogul, nor any of the others, possessed any thing equal to it. " Behold the *Catholic Church!*" said the angel. " Is it here that Emmanuel keeps his court?" said I. " Yes," he replied, " this is his only terrestrial palace." " Has he any crowned heads under him?" said I. " A few," was the answer. " There are your good queen Anne, and some princes of Denmark and Germany, and a few of the other small princes." " What are they," said I, " compared with those who are under Belial the Great? He has emperors and kings without number." "Notwithstanding all this," said the angel, "not one of them can move a finger without the permission of Emmanuel, nor Belial himself either, because Emmanuel is his lawful king; Belial rebelled, and for his rebellion was made a captive, with permission however to visit for a little time the city of Perdition, and delude any one he could into his own rebellion and a share of his punishment. So great is his malice, that he is continually using this permission, though aware that by so doing he will only add to his own misery; and so great is his love of wickedness, that he takes advantage of his half liberty, to seek to destroy this city and this edifice, though he has long known that their guardian is invincible."

"Pray, my lord," said I, "may we approach and take a more minute view of this magnificent palace?" for my heart had warmed towards the place at the first sight. "Certainly you may," said the angel, "because there I have my place, charge, and employment." The nearer we went to it, the more I wondered, seeing how lofty, strong, beautiful, pure, and lovely every part of it was; how accurate was the workmanship, and how fair were its materials. A rock wrought with immense labour, and of prodigious strength was the foundation stone; living stones were placed upon this rock, and were cemented in so admirable a manner, that it was impossible for one stone to be so beautiful in another place, as it was in its own. I could see one part of the *church* which cast out a very fair and remarkable cross, and the angel perceiving me gazing upon it, asked me "if I knew that part." I did not know what to answer. "That is the *Church of England*," said he. These words made me observe it with more attention than before, and on looking up I could perceive queen Anne, on the pinnacle of the building, with a sword in each hand. With the one in her left, which is called Justice, she preserves her subjects from the men of the city of Perdition; and with the other in her right, which is the sword of the Spirit, or the word of God, she preserves them from Belial and his spiritual evils. Under the left sword were the *Laws of England:* under the other was a large *Bible.* The sword of the Spirit was fiery and of prodigious length, it would kill at a distance to which the other sword could not reach. I observed the other princes with the same arms, defending their portions of the church; but I could see that the portion of my queen was the fairest, and that her arms were the most bright. By her right hand, I could see a multitude of people in black—archbishops, bishops, and teachers, assisting her in sustaining the sword of the Spirit; and some of the soldiers and civil officers, and a few, very few of the lawyers, supporting, along with her, the other sword. I obtained permission to rest a little by one of the magnificent doors, whither people were coming to obtain the dignity of the *universal church:* a tall angel was keeping the door, and the church within side was so vividly light, that it was useless for *Hypocrisy* to show her visage there—she sometimes appeared at the door, but never went in. After I had been gazing about a quarter of an hour, there came a *papist*, who imagined that the Pope possessed the catholic church, and he claimed his share of dignity. "What proof of your dignity have you?" said the porter. "I have plenty," said he, "of *traditions of the fathers,* and *acts of the congresses of the church;* but what further assurance do I need, than the word of the Pope, who sits upon the infallible chair?" Then the porter proceeded to open an exceedingly large Bible. "Behold,"

said he, "the only Statute Book which we use here, prove
your claim out of that, or depart;" whereupon he departed.

At this moment there came a drove of Quakers, who
wanted to go in with their hats upon their heads, but they
were turned back for their unmannerly behaviour. After that,
some of the children of the barn, who had been there for some
time, began to speak. "We have," said they, "no other
statute than you, therefore show us our dignity." "Stay,"
said the glittering porter, looking them fixedly in the face,
" and I will show you something. Do you see yonder," said he,
" the rent which you made in the church, that you might go
out of it, without the slightest cause or reason? and now,
what do you want here? Go back to the narrow gate, wash
yourselves well in the fountain of repentance, in order to free
yourselves from some of the kingly blood, in which you steeped
yourselves formerly; bring some of that water to moisten the
clay, to close up the rent yonder, and then, and then only, you
shall be welcome." But before we had proceeded a rood farther towards the west, we heard a buzz amongst the princes
above, and every one, great and small, seized his arms, and
proceeded to harness himself as if for battle; and before we had
time to espy a place to flee to, the whole air became dark, and
the city was more deeply over-shadowed than during an
eclipse; the thunder began to roar, and the lightnings to dart
forkedly, and a ceaseless shower of mortal arrows, was directed
from the gates below, against the catholic church; and unless
every one had had a shield in his hand to receive the fiery
darts, and unless the foundation stone had been too strong for
any thing to make an impression upon it, you would have
seen the whole in conflagration. But alas! this was but the
prologue, or a foretaste of what was to follow; for the dark-

ness speedily became seven times blacker, and *Belial* himself appeared upon the densest cloud, and around him were his choicest warriors, both terrestrial and infernal, to receive and execute his will, on their particular sides. He had enjoined the Pope, and the king of France, his other son, to destroy the church of England and its queen; and the Turk and the Muscovite, to break to pieces the other parts of the Church, and to slay the people; the queen and the other princes, were by no means to be spared; and the Bible was to be burned in spite of every thing. The first thing which the queen and the other saints did, was to fall upon their knees, and complain of their wrongs to the King of kings, in these words: —" *The spreading of his wings covereth the extent of thy land, O Emmanuel!*" Isaiah 8. iii. This complaint was answered by a voice, which said, "*resist the devil and he will flee from you;*" and then ensued the hardest and most stubborn engagement, which had ever been upon the earth. When the *sword of the Spirit* began to be waved, Belial and his infernal legions began to retreat, and the Pope to falter. The king of France, it is true, held out; yet even he nearly lost heart, for he saw the queen and her subjects united and prosperous, whilst his own ships were sunk, his soldiers slaughtered, and thousands of his subjects rebelling. The very Turk was becoming as gentle as a lamb; but just at that moment my heavenly associate quitted me, darting up towards the firmament, to myriads of other shining powers, and my dream was at an end. Yes, just as the Pope and the other terrestrial powers, were beginning to sneak away, and to faint, and the potentates of hell to fall by tens of thousands, each making, to my imagination's ear, as much noise as if a huge mountain had been precipitated into the depths of the sea, my companion quitted me, and there was an end of my dream; for what with the noise made by the fiends, and the agitation which I felt at losing my companion, I awoke from my sleep, and returned with the utmost reluctance to my sluggish clod, thinking how noble and delightful it was to be a *free* spirit, to wander about in angelic company, quite secure, though seemingly in the midst of peril. I had now nothing to console me, save the Muse, and she being half angry, would do nothing more than bleat to me the following strains.

The Perishing World.

O man, upon this building gaze,
The mansion of the human race,
The world terrestrial see!
Its architect's the King on high,
Who ne'er was born and ne'er will die—
The blest Divinity.
The world, its wall, its starlights all,
Its stores, where'er they lie,
Its wondrous brute variety,
Its reptiles, fish, and birds that fly,

And cannot number'd be,
The God above, to show his love,
Did give, O man, to thee.
For man, for man, whom he did plan,
God caus'd arise
This edifice,
Equal to heaven in all but size,
Beneath the sun so fair:
Then it he view'd, and that 'twas good
For man, he was aware.

Man only sought to know at first
Evil, and of the thing accursed
Obtain a sample small.
The sample grew a giantess,
'Tis easy from her size to guess
The whole her prey will fall.
Cellar and turret high,
Through hell's dark treachery,
Now reeling, rocking terribly,
In swooning pangs appear;
The orchards round, are only found
Vile sedge and weeds to bear;
The roof gives way, more, more each day,
The walls too, spite
Of all their might,
Have frightful cracks, down all their height,
Which coming ruin show;
The dragons tell, that danger fell,
Now lurks the house below.

O man! this building fair and proud,
From its foundation to the cloud,
Is all in dangerous plight:
Beneath thee quakes and shakes the ground:
'Tis all, e'en down to hell's profound,
A bog that scares the sight.
The sin man wrought, the deluge brought,
And without fail
A fiery gale,
Before which every thing shall quail,
His deeds shall waken now;
Worse evermore, till all is o'er,
Thy case, O world, shall grow.
There's one place free, yet, man for thee,
Where mercies reign,
A place to which thou may'st attain,
Seek there a residence to gain
Lest thou in caverns howl;
For save thou there shalt quick repair,
Woe to thy wretched soul!

Towards yon building turn your face!
Too strong by far is yonder place
To lose the victory.
'Tis better than the reeling world;
For all the ills by hell uphurl'd
It has a remedy.
Sublime it braves the wildest waves;
It is a refuge place
Impregnable to Belial's race,
With stones, emitting vivid rays,

Above its stately porch;
Itself, and those therein, compose
The universal church.
Though slaves of sin we long have been,
With faith sincere
We shall win pardon there;
Then in let's press, O, brethren dear,
And claim our dignity!
By doing so, we saints below
And saints on high shall be.

A Vision of Death in his Palace Below.

In one of the long, black, chilly nights of winter, when it was much warmer in a kitchen of Glyn-cywarch, than on the summit of Cadair Idris, and much more pleasant to be in a snug chamber, with a warm bed-fellow, than in a shroud in the church yard, I was musing upon some discourses which had passed between me and a neighbour, upon *the shortness of human life,* and how certain every one is of dying, and how uncertain as to the time. Whilst thus engaged, having but newly laid my head down upon the pillow, and being about half awake, I felt a great weight coming stealthily upon me, from the crown of my head to my heel, so that I could not stir a finger, nor any thing except my tongue, and beheld a lad upon my breast, and a lass mounted upon his back. On looking sharply, I guessed, from the warm smell which came from him, his clammy locks, and his gummy eyes, that the lad must be *master Sleep.* "Pray, sir," said I, squealing, "what have I done to you, that you bring that witch here to suffocate me?" "Hush," said he, "it is only my sister *Nightmare;*

we are both going to visit our brother *Death*, and have
need of a third, and lest you should resist, we have come
upon you without warning, as he himself will sometime;
therefore you must come, whether you will or not." " Alas!"
said I, " must I die?" " O no," said *Nightmare*; " we will
spare you this time." " But with your favour," said I, " your
brother Death never spared any one yet who was brought
within reach of his dart; the fellow even ventured to fling a
fall with the Lord of Life himself, though it is true he gained
very little by his daring." At these words *Nightmare* arose
full of wrath and departed. " Hey," said *Sleep*, " come away,
and you shall have no cause to repent of your journey."
" Well," said I, " may there never be night to *saint Sleep*, and
may *Nightmare* never obtain any other place to crouch upon
than the top of an awl, unless you return me to where you
found me." Then away he went with me, over woods and
precipices, over oceans and valleys, over castles and towers,
rivers and crags; and where did we descend, but by one of the
gates of the daughters of Belial, on the posterior side of the
city of Perdition, and I could there perceive, that the three
gates of Perdition contracted into one on the hinder side, and
opened into the same place—a place foggy, cold, and pesti-
lential, replete with an unwholesome vapour, and clouds
lowering and terrible. " Pray, sir," said I, " what dungeon
of a place is this?" " *The chambers of Death*," said *Sleep*.
I had scarcely time to enquire, before I heard some people
crying, some screaming, some groaning, some talking deliri-
ously, some uttering blasphemies in a feeble tone; others in
great agony, as if about to give up the ghost. Here and
there one, after a mighty shout would become silent, and
then forthwith I could hear a key revolving in a lock; I

turned at the sound to look for the door, and by dint of long gazing, I could see tens of thousands of doors, apparently far off, though close by my side notwithstanding. "Please to inform me, master Sleep," said I, "to what place these doors open?" "They open," he replied, "into the *land of Oblivion*, a vast country under the rule of my brother Death; and the great wall here, is the limit of the immense eternity." As I looked I could see a little death at each door, all with differ-ent arms, and different names, though evidently they were all subjects of the same king. Notwithstanding which, there was much contention between them concerning the sick; for the one wished to snatch the sick through his door, and the other would fain have him through his own. On drawing near, we could see above every door, the name of the death written, who kept it; and likewise by every door, hundreds of various things left scattered about, denoting the haste of those who went through. Over one door I could see *Famine*, though purses and full bags were lying on the ground beside it, and boxes nailed up, standing near. "That," said he, "is the gate of the *misers*." "To whom," said I, "do these rags belong?" "Principally to misers," he replied; "but there are some there belonging to lazy idlers, and to ballad singers, and to others, poor in every thing, but spirit, who preferred starvation to begging." In the next door was the death of the *Ruling Passion*, and parallel with it I could hear many voices, as of men in the extremity of cold. By this door were many books, some pots and flaggons, here and there a staff and a walking stick, some compasses and charts, and shipping tackle. "This is the road by which scholars go," said I. "Some scholars go by it," said he, "solitary, helpless wretches, whose relations have stripped them of their last

article of raiment; but people of various other descriptions go
by it also. Those," said he, (speaking of the pots,) "are the
relics of jolly companions, whose feet are freezing under
benches, whilst their heads are boiling with drink and uproar;
and the things yonder belong to travellers of snowy mountains,
and to traffickers in the North sea."

Next at hand was a meagre skeleton of a figure, called
the *death of Fear*. Through his exterior you might see that
he did not possess any heart: and by his door there were
bags, and chests also, and locks, and castles. By this gate
went usurers, bad governors and tyrants, and some of the
murderers, but the plurality of the latter were driven past
to the next gate, where there was a death called *Gallows*,
with his cord ready for their necks.

Next was to be seen the *death of Love*, and by his feet
were hundreds of instruments, and books of music, and
verses, and love letters, and also ointments and colors to
beautify the countenance, and a thousand other embellishing
wares, and also some swords. "With some of those swords,"
said my companion, "bandits have been slain whilst fighting
for women, and with others, love-lorn creatures have stabbed
themselves." I could perceive that this death was purblind.

At the next door, was a death who had the most repul-
sive figure of all; his entire liver was consumed. He was
called the *death of Envy*. "This one," said Sleep, "assaults
losing gamesters, slanderers, and many a female rider, who
repineth at the law which rendered the wife subject to her
husband." "Pray, sir," said I, "what is the meaning of
female rider?" "Female rider," said he, "is the term used
here, for the woman who would ride her husband, her neigh-

bours, and her country too, if possible, and the end of her long riding will be, that she will ride the Devil, from that door, down to hell."

Next stood the door of the *death of Ambition*, and of those who lift their nostrils on high, and break their shins for want of looking beneath their feet. Beside this door were crowns, sceptres, banners, all sorts of patents and commissions, and all kinds of heraldric and warlike arms.

But before I could look on any more of these countless doors, I heard a voice commanding me by my name to prepare. At this word, I could feel myself beginning to melt, like a snow ball in the heat of the sun; whereupon my master gave me some soporific drink, so that I fell asleep, but by the time I awoke, he had conveyed me to a considerable distance, on the other side of the wall. I found myself in a valley of pitchy darkness, and as it seemed to me, limitless. At the end of a little time, I could see by a dim light, like that of a dying candle, innumerable human shades—some on foot, and some on horseback, running through one another like the wind, silently and with wonderful solemnity.

It was a desert, bare, and blasted country, without grass, or vegetation, or woods, and without animals, with the exception of deadly monsters, and venemous reptiles of every kind; serpents, snakes, lice, toads, maw-worms, locusts, earwigs, and the like, which all exist on human corruption. Through myriads of shades, and creeping things, graves, sepulchres, and cemeteries, we proceeded, without interruption, to observe the country. At last I perceived some of the shades turning and looking upon me; and suddenly, notwithstanding the great silence that had prevailed before, there was a whispering from one to the other that there was a *living man* at hand. "A living man," said one; "a living man," said the other; and they came thronging about me like caterpillars from every corner. "How did you come hither, sirrah?" said a little morkin of a death who was there. "Truly, sir," said I, "I know no more than yourself." "What do they call you?" he demanded. "Call me what you please, here in your own country," I replied, "but at home I am called *the Sleeping Bard.*"

At that word I beheld a crooked old man, with a double head like to a rough-barked thorn tree, raising himself erect, and looking upon me worse than the black devil himself; and lo! without saying a word, he hurled a large human skull at my head—many thanks to a tombstone which shielded me. "Pray be quiet, sir," said I, "I am but a stranger, who was never here before, and you may be sure I will never return, if I can once reach home again." "I will give you cause to remember having been here," said he; and attacked me with a thigh-bone, like a very devil, whilst I avoided his blows as well as I could. "By heavens," said I, "this is a most inhospitable country to strangers. Is there a justice of the peace here?" "Peace!" said he, "what peace do you deserve, who will not let people rest in their graves?" "Pray, sir," said I, "may I be allowed to know your name, because I am not aware of ever having disturbed any one in this country." "Sirrah," said he, "know that not you are the Sleeping Bard, but that I am that person; and I have been allowed to rest here for nine hundred years, by every one but yourself." And he attacked me again.

"Forbear, my brother," said Merddyn, who was near at hand, "be not too hot; rather be thankful to him for keeping an honorable remembrance of your name upon earth." "Great

honor, forsooth," said he, "I shall receive from such a blockhead as this. Sirrah! can you sing in the four-and-twenty
measures? Can you carry the pedigree of Gog and Magog,
and the genealogy of Brutus ap Sylfius, up to a millenium
previous to the fall of Troy? Can you narrate when, and what
will be the end of the combats betwixt the lion and the eagle,
and betwixt the dragon and the red deer?" "Hey, hey! let
me ask him a question," said another, who was seated beside
a large cauldron which was boiling, and going, bubble, bubble,
over a fire. "Come nearer," said he, "what is the meaning
of this?"

> "I till the judgment day
> Upon the earth shall stray;
> None knows for certainty
> Whether fish or flesh I be."

"I will request the favor of your name, sir," said I, "that I
may answer you in a suitable manner." "I," said he, "am
Taliesin,‡ the prince of the Bards of the West, and that is a

‡ Taliesin lived in the sixth century; he was a foundling, discovered
in his infancy lying in a coracle, on a salmon-weir, in the domain of
Elphin, a prince of North Wales, who became his patron. During his
life he arrogated to himself a supernatural descent and understanding,
and for at least a thousand years after his death he was regarded by the
descendants of the Ancient Britons, as a prophet or something more.
The poems which he produced procured for him the title of "Bardic
King;" they display much that is vigorous and original, but are dis-
figured by mysticism and extravagant metaphor. The four lines which
he is made to quote above are from his Hanes, or History, one of the
most spirited of his pieces. When Elis Wynn represents him as sitting
by a cauldron in Hades, he alludes to a wild legend concerning him, to
the effect, that he imbibed awen or poetical genius whilst employed in
watching "the seething pot" of the sorceress Cridwen, which legend has
much in common with one of the Irish legends about Fin Macoul, which
is itself nearly identical with one in the Edda, describing the manner
in which Sigurd Fafnisbane became possessed of supernatural wisdom.

piece of my composition." "I know not," said I, "what could
be your meaning, unless it was, that the yellow plague§ which
destroyed Maelgwn of Gwynedd, put an end to you on the
sea-shore, and that your body was divided amongst the crows
and the fishes." "Peace, fool!" said he, "I was alluding to
my two callings, of man of the law and poet. Please to tell
me, has a lawyer more similitude to a raven, than a poet to a
whale? How many a one doth a single lawyer divest of his
flesh, to swell out his own craw; and with what indifference
does he extract the blood, and leave a man half alive! And
as for the poet, where is the fish which is able to swallow like
him? he is drinking oceans of liquor at all times, but the briny
sea itself would not slack his thirst. And provided a man be
a poet and a lawyer, how is it possible to know whether he be
fish or flesh, especially if he be a courtier to boot, as I was,
and obliged to vary his taste to every ones palate. But tell
me," said he, "whether there are at present, any of those
fellows upon the earth?" "There's plenty of them," said I;
"if one can patch together any nonsensical derry, he is styled
a graduate bard. But as for the others; there is such a
plague of lawyers, petty attornies, and scribes, that the locusts
of Egypt bore light upon the country, in comparison with
them. In your time, sir, there were but bargains of tofts and
crofts, and a hand's breadth of writing for a farm of a hundred
pounds, and a raising of cairns and crosses, as memorials of
the purchase and boundaries. There is no longer any such
security, but there is far more craft and deceit, and a tombstone's breadth of written parchment to secure the bargain;

§ A dreadful pestilence, which ravaged Gwynedd or North Wales
in 560. Amongst its victims was the king of the country, the celebrated Maelgwn, son of Caswallon Law Hir.

and for all that, it is a wonder if a flaw be not in it, or said to
be at least." "Well then," said Taliesin, "I should not be
worth a straw in the world at present, I am better where I am.
Truth will never be had where there are many poets, nor fair
dealing where there are many lawyers; no, nor health where
there are many physicians." At this moment, a little grey-
headed hobgoblin, who had heard that a living man was
arrived, flung himself at my feet, weeping abundantly. "Dear
me," said I, "what are you?" "One who is grievously wronged
every day in the world," said he. "May God move your soul
to procure justice for me." "What is your name?" said I.
"I am called *Somebody*," he replied, "and there is scarcely a
piece of pimping, or a calumny, or a lie, or tale, to set people
at loggerheads, but must be laid upon me. 'Verily,' says one,
'she is a prodigious fine girl, and she was praising you before
somebody, notwithstanding that some very great person is
paying his suit to her.' 'I heard somebody,' says another,
'reckoning that this estate was mortgaged nine hundred
pounds deep.' 'I saw some one yesterday,' says the beggar,
'with a chequered slop, like a sailor, who had come with a
large ship load of corn, to the neighbouring port.' And thus
every ragged dog mangles me for his own wicked purposes.
Some call me Friend—'I was informed by a friend,' says one,
'that so and so has no intention of leaving a farthing to his
wife, and that there is no affection between them.' Some
others vilify me yet more, and call me Bird—'A bird whistled
in my ear, that there are bad practices going on there,' say
they. It is true, some call me by the more respectable name
of Old Person; yet, not half the omens, prophecies, and
counsels, which are attributed to the Old Person, belong to
me. I have never bidden people to follow the old road,

provided the new one be better, nor a hundred similar things. But Somebody is my common name," he continued, "him you will most frequently hear, to have been concerned in every atrocious matter. Because, ask a person wherever a vile, slanderous falsehood has been uttered, who it was who said it, and he will reply, 'Truly I don't know who, but somebody in the company said it;' question then every one in the company concerning the fable, and every one will say he heard it from somebody, but no one knows from whom. Is not this a shameful injury?" he demanded. "Be so good as to inform every one whom you may hear naming me, that I have never said any one of these things, nor have ever invented nor uttered a lie to slander any one, nor a story to set relations by the ears; that I do not go near them; that I know nothing of their history, nor of their affairs, nor of their accursed secrets; and that they ought not to fling their wickedness upon me, but on their own corrupt brains."

At this moment there came a little death, one of the secretaries of the king, desiring to know my name, and commanding master Sleep, to carry me instantly before the king. I was compelled to go, though utterly against my will, by the power, which, like a whirlwind carried me away, betwixt high and low, thousands of miles back to the left hand, until we came again in sight of the boundary wall, and reached a narrow corner. Here we perceived an immense, frowning, ruinous palace, open at the top, reaching to the wall where were the innumerable doors, all of which led to this huge, terrific court. The walls were constructed with the sculls of men, which grinned horribly with their teeth. The clay was black, and was prepared with tears and sweat; and the mortar on the outside was variegated with phlegm and pus, and on the inside with black-red blood. On the top of each turret, you might see a little death, with a smoking heart stuck on the point of his dart.

Around the palace was a wood, consisting of a few poisonous yews and deadly cypresses, and in these, owls, blood crows, vultures and the like were nestling, and croaking continually for flesh, though the whole place was nothing but a stinking shamble. We entered the gate. All the pillars of the hall were made of human thigh bones; the pillars of the parlour were of shank bones; and the floors were one continued layer of every species of offal. It was not long before I came in sight of a vast and frightful altar, where I beheld the king of Terrors swallowing human flesh and blood, and a thousand petty deaths, from every hole, feeding him with fresh, warm flesh. "Behold," said the death who brought me there, addressing himself to the king, "a spark, whom I found in the midst of the land of Oblivion; he came so light footed, that your majesty never tasted a morsel of him." "How can that be?" said the king, and opened his jaws as wide as an earth-quake to swallow me. Whereupon I turned all trembling to Sleep. "It was I," said Sleep, "who brought him here." "Well," said the meagre, grizly king, turning to me, "for my brother Sleep's sake, you shall be permitted to return this time, but beware of me the next." After having employed himself for a considerable time in casting carcasses into his insatiable paunch, he caused his subjects to be called together, and moved from the altar to a terrific throne of exceeding height, to pronounce judgment on the prisoners newly arrived. In an instant came innumerable multitudes of the dead, making their obeisance to their king, and taking their stations in remarkable order. And lo! king Death was in his regal vest of flaming scarlet, covered all over with figures of women and children weeping, and men uttering groans; about his head was a black-red three-cornered cap, (which his friend Lucifer had sent as a present to him,) and upon its corners were written *misery, wailing,* and *woe.* Above his head were thousands of representations of battles on sea and land, towns burning, the earth opening, and the great water of the deluge; and beneath his feet nothing was to be seen but the crowns and sceptres of the kings whom he had overcome from the beginning. On his right hand *Fate* was sitting, seemingly engaged in reading, with a murky look, a huge volume which was before him; and on his left was an old man called *Time,* licking innumerable threads of gold, and silver, and copper, and very many of iron. Some few of the threads were growing better towards their end, and thousands growing worse. Along the threads were hours, days, and years; and Fate, according as his volume directed him, was continually breaking the threads of life, and opening the doors of the boundary wall, betwixt the two worlds.

We had not looked around us long, before we heard four fiddlers, newly dead, summoned to the bar. "How comes it," said the king of Terrors, "that loving merriment as ye do, ye kept not on the other side of the gulf, for there has never been any merriment on this side." "We have never done," said one of the musicians, "harm to any body, but have rendered people joyous, and have taken quietly what they gave us for our pains." Said Death, "did you never keep any one from his work, and cause him to lose his time; or did you never keep people from church? ha!" "O no!" said another, perhaps now and then on a Sunday, after service, we may have kept some in the public house till the next morning, or during summer tide, may have kept them dancing in the ring on the green all night; for sure enough, we were more liked, and more lucky in obtaining a congregation than the parson." "Away, away with these fellows to the country of Despair!" said the terrific king, "bind the four back to back and cast them to their customers, to dance bare-footed on floors of glowing heat, and to amble to all eternity without either praise or music."

The next that came to the bar was a certain king, who had lived very near to Rome. "Hold up your hand, prisoner," said one of the officers. " I hope," said he, " that you have some better manners and favour to show to a king." "Sirrah," said Death, "why did you not keep on the other side of the gulf where all are kings? On this side there is none but myself, and another down below, and you will soon see, that neither he nor I will rate you according to the degree of your majesty, but according to the degree of your wickedness, in order to adapt your punishment to your crimes, therefore answer to the interrogation." "Sir," he replied, "I would have you know, that you have no authority to detain me, nor to interrogate me, as I have a pardon for all my sins under the Pope's own hand. On account of my faithful services, he has given me a warrant to go straight to Paradise, without tarrying one moment in Purgatory." At these words the king and all the haggard train gave a ghastly grin, to escape from laughing outright; but the other full of wrath at their ridicule, commanded them aloud to show him the way. "Peace, thou lost fool!" cried Death, Purgatory lies behind you, on the other side of the wall, for you ought to purify yourself during your life; and on the right hand, on the other side of that gulf is Paradise. But there is no road by which it is possible for you to escape, either through the gulf to Paradise, or through the boundary wall back to the world; and if you were to give your kingdom, (supposing you could give it,) you would not obtain permission from the keepers of those doors, to take one peep through the key hole.   It is called the irrepassable wall, for when once you have come through you may abandon all hope of returning. But since you stand so high on the books of the Pope, you shall go and pre-pare his bed, beside that of the Pope who was before him, and there you shall kiss his toe for ever, and he the toe of Lucifer."

Immediately thereupon, four little deaths raised the poor king up, who was by this time shivering like the leaf of an aspen, and snatched him out of sight like lightning. Next after him came a young fellow and woman. He had been a jolly companion and she a lady of pleasure, or one free of her person ; but they were called here by their naked names, drunkard and harlot. " I hope," said the drunkard, " I shall find some favour with you; I have sent to you many a bloated booty in a torrent of good ale; and when I failed to kill others, I came myself, willingly, to feed you."   " With the permission of the court," said the harlot, "you have not sent half as much as I, and my offerings were burning sacri-fices, rich roast meat ready for the board."   " Hey, hey!" said Death, "all this was done for your own accursed passions' sake and not to feed me.   Bind the two face to face, as they are old acquaintances, and cast them into the land of Darkness, and let each be a torment to the other, until the day of judgment." They were then snatched away, with their heads downwards.

Next to these there came seven recorders. Having been commanded to raise their hands to the bar, they would by no means obey, as the rails were greasy. One began to wrangle boisterously; "we ought to obtain a fair citation to prepare our answer," said he, "instead of being rushed upon unawares."

"But are we bound to give you that same specific citation," answered Death, "since you obtain in every place, and at every period of your life, warning of my coming. How many sermons have you not heard upon the mortality of man? How many books have you not seen? How many graves, how many sculls, how many diseases, how many messages and signs have you not had? What is your Sleep, but my own brother? What are sculls, but my visage? What does your daily food consist of but dead creatures? Seek not to cast your neglect upon me. Speak not of summons, when you have obtained it a hundred times." "Pray," said one red recorder, "what have you to advance against us?" "What?" said Death. "Drinking the sweat and blood of the poor, and levying double your wages." "Here is an honest man," replied the recorder, pointing to a pettifogger behind him, "who knows that we have never done any thing but what was fair; and it is not fair of you to detain us here, without a specific crime to prove against us." "Hey, hey!" said Death, "you shall prove against yourselves. Place these people," said he, "on the verge of the *precipice* before the tribunal of *Justice*, they shall obtain equity there though they never practiced it."

There were still seven other prisoners remaining, and these kept up a prodigious bustle and noise. Some were flattering, others quarrelling, some blustering, some counseling, &c. Scarcely had they been called to the bar, when lo! the entire palace became seven times more horribly dark than before, and there was a shivering and a great agitation about the throne, and Death became paler than ever. Upon enquiring what was the matter, one of the messengers of Lucifer stepped forward with a letter for Death, concerning these seven prisoners, and Fate presently caused the letter to be read publicly, and these were the words, as far as I can remember.

"*Lucifer, King of the kings of the world, prince of Hell, and chief ruler of the Deep, to our natural son, the most mighty and terrible king Death, greeting, pre-eminence, and eternal spoil.*

"For as much as we have been informed by some of our nimble messengers, who are constantly abroad to obtain information, that seven prisoners, of the seven most villainous and dangerous species in the world, have arrived lately at your royal palace, and that it is your intention to hurl them over the cliff into my kingdom. I hereby counsel you to try every possible means, to let them loose back again upon the world; they will do you there more service in sending you food, and sending me better company, for I would rather want than have them; we have had but too much plague with their companions for a long time, and my dominion is still disturbed by them. Therefore turn them back, or keep them with you. For, by the infernal crown, if you send them here, I will undermine the foundations of your kingdom, until it falls down into my own immense dominion.

"*From the burning hall of assembly, at our royal palace in the pit of Hell, in the year of our reign, 5425.*"

King Death, hereupon, stood for some time with his visage green and pale, in great perplexity of mind. But whilst he was meditating, behold *Fate* turned upon him such an iron-black scowl, as made him tremble. "Sirrah," said he, "look to what you do. It is not in my power to send any one back, through the boundary of eternity, the irrepassable wall, nor in yours to harbour them here; therefore forward them to their destruction, in spite of the Arch Fiend. He has been able hitherto, in a minute to allot his proper place to every individual, in a drove of a thousand, nay, even of ten thousand captured souls: and what difficulty can he have with seven, however dangerous they may be. But though these seven should turn the infernal government topsy-turvy, do you drive them thither instantly, for fear I should receive commands to annihilate you before your time. As for *his* threats, they are only lies; for although thy end, and that of the old man yonder, (looking at Time,) are nigh at hand, being written only a few pages further on, in my unerring volume, yet you have no cause to be afraid of sinking to Lucifer; though every one in the abyss would be glad to obtain thee, yet they never, never shall. For the rocks of steel and eternal adamant, which form the roof of Hell, are too strong for anything to crumble them." Whereupon, Death, considerably startled, called to one of his train, to write for him the following answer.

"*Death, the king of Terror and Conqueror of conquerors, to his revered friend and neighbour Lucifer, king of Eternal Night, sovereign of the Bottomless Pool, sends greeting.*

"After due reflection on your regal desire, it has appeared to us more advantageous, not only to our own dominion, but likewise to your own extensive kingdom, to send these

prisoners, as far as possible from the doors of the irrepassable
wall, lest their putrid odour should terrify the whole city of
Destruction, so that no man should come to all eternity, to
my side of the gate; and neither I obtain any thing to cool
my sting, nor you a concourse of customers from earth to hell.
Therefore I will leave to you to judge them, and to hurl them
into such cells, as you may deem the most proper and secure
for them.

> "*From my nether palace in the great gate of Perdition, over
> Destruction.   In the year, from the renewal of my
> kingdom,* 1670."

At hearing all this, I felt a great curiosity to know who
these seven people could be, whom the devils themselves held
in so much dread.   But ere a minute had elapsed, the clerk
of the crown called their names, as follows:—Master Meddler,
alias *Finger in Every Dish*; but he was so vehement and
busy in advising the others, that he could not get a moment's
time to answer for himself, until Death threatened to transfix
him with his dart.

Then *master Slanderer* was called, alias *Enemy of Fair
Fame*; but there was no answer.   "He is too modest to hear
his titles," said the third, "and he never can bear his nicknames."   "Do you suppose," said the *Slanderer*, "that you
yourself have no *titles*.   Call for," said he, "*master Coxcomb,
alias Smooth Gullet*, alias *Poison Smile*."   "Ready," said a
woman who was there, pointing to the Coxcomb.   "O," said
he, "*madam Bouncer!*   Your humble servant, I am overjoyed
at seeing you well.   I have never seen a woman look handsomer
in breeches.   But, oh! to think how miserable the country
must be behind you, for want of its admirable she-governor;

yet your delightful company will make hell itself something better." "O son of the arch fiend!" said she. "With you there is no need of another hell, you are yourself enough." Then the cryer called *Bouncer*, or *mistress Breeches*. "Ready," said another. But she said not a word, for want of being called madam. Next was called *Contriver of Contrivances*, alias *Jack of all Trades*; but he returned no answer either, for he was busied in devising a way to escape. "Ready, ready," said one behind, "here he is, looking out for an opportunity to break through your palace, and unless you take care, he will have some notable contrivance to baulk you." Said the Contriver, "call him, I beseech you, *master Impeacher of his Brother*, alias *Searcher of Faults*, alias *Framer of Complaints*." "Ready, ready, this is he," said a litigious pettifogger, for every one knew the name of the other, but would not acknowledge his own. "You shall be called," said the Impeacher, "*master Litigious Pettifogger*, alias *the Courts Comprised*." "Bear witness, I pray you all," said the Pettifogger, "as to what the knave called me." "Ho, ho!" said Death, "not by the baptismal font, but by his sins, is every one called in this country; and, with your permission, master Pettifogger, the names of your sins are those which shall stick to you henceforth for ever." "Hey," said the Pettifogger, "I swear by the Devil that I will make you smart for this. Though you are empowered to kill me, you have no authority to bestow nicknames upon me. I will file a complaint against you for defamation, and another for false imprisonment, against you and your friend Lucifer, in the court of Justice."

By this time, I beheld the legions of Death, formed in order and armed, with their eyes fixed upon the king, awaiting the word. "There," said the king, standing erect upon his regal throne, "my terrible and invincible hosts, spare neither care nor diligence in removing these prisoners from out of my boundaries, lest they prove the ruin of my country; cast them bound, over the precipice of Despair, with their heads downward. But for the seventh, this Courts Comprised, who threatens me, leave him free over the chasm, beneath the court of *Justice*, and let him try whether he can make his complaint good against me." Then Death reseated himself. And lo! all the deadly legions, after surrounding the prisoners and binding them, led them away to their couch. I also went out, and peeped after them. "Come away," said Sleep, and snatched me up to the top of the highest turret of the palace. Thence I could see the prisoners proceeding to their eternal perdition. Presently a whirlwind arose, and dispersed the pitch-black cloud, which was spread universally over the face of the land of Oblivion, and by the light of a thousand candles, which were burning with a blue flame, at a particular place, I obtained a far distant view of the verge of the *Bottomless Gulf*, a sight exceedingly horrible; and also of a spectacle above, still more appaling, namely *Justice* upon his *supreme seat*, holding the keys of Hell, at a separate and distinct tribunal over the chasm, to pronounce judgment upon the damned as they came. I could see the prisoners cast headlong down the gulf, and Pettifogger rushing to fling himself over the terrific brink, rather than look once on the court of *Justice*. For oh! there was there a spectacle too severe for a guilty countenance. I merely gazed from *afar*, but I beheld more terrific horror, than I can at present relate, or I could at that time support, for my spirit struggled and fluttered at the awful sight, and wrestled so strenuously, that it burst all the bands of Sleep, and my soul returned to its accustomed functions. And exceedingly overjoyed I was to see myself still amongst the living. I instantly determined upon reforming myself, as a hundred years of affliction in the paths of righteousness, would be less harrowing to me, than another glance on the horrors of this night.

Death the Great.

Leave land and house we must some day,
For human sway not long doth bide;
Leave pleasures and festivities,
And pedigrees, our boast and pride.

Leave strength and loveliness of mien,
Wit sharp and keen, experience dear;
Leave learning deep, and much lov'd friends,
And all that tends our life to cheer.

From Death then is there no relief?
That ruthless thief and murderer fell,
Who to his shambles beareth down
All, all we own, and us as well.

Ye monied men, ye who would fain
Your wealth retain eternally,
How brave 'twould be a sum to raise,
And the good grace of Death to buy !

How brave ! ye who with beauty beam,
On rank supreme who fix your mind,
Should ye your captivations muster,
And with their lustre king Death blind.

O ye who are at foot most light,
Who are in the height now of your spring,
Fly, fly, and ye will make us gape,
If ye can scape Death's cruel fling.

The song and dance afford, I ween,
Relief from spleen, and sorrows grave;
How very strange there is no dance,
Nor tune of France, from Death can save !

Ye travellers of sea and land,
Who know each strand below the sky ;
Declare if ye have seen a place,
Where Adam's race can Death defy !

Ye scholars, and ye lawyer crowds,
Who are as gods reputed wise;
Can ye from all the lore ye know,
Gainst Death bestow some good advice?

The world, the flesh, and Devil, compose
The direst foes of mortals poor;
But take good heed of Death the Great,
From the Lost Gate, Destruction o'er.

'Tis not worth while of Death to prate,
Of his Lost Gate and courts so wide;.
But O reflect! it much imports,
Of the two courts in which ye're tried.

It here can little signify
If the street high we cross, or low;
Each lofty thought doth rise, be sure.
The soul to lure to deepest woe.

But by the wall that's ne'er re-pass'd.
To gripe thee fast when Death prepares,
Heed, heed thy steps, for thou mayst mourn
The slightest turn for endless years.

When opes the door, and swiftly hence
To its residence eternal flies
The soul, it matters much, which side
Of the gulf wide its journey lies.

Deep penitence, amended life,
A bosom rife of zeal and faith,
Can help to man alone impart,
Against the smart and sting of Death.

These things to thee seem worthless now,
But not so low will they appear
When thou art come. O thoughtless friend!
Just to the end of thy career.

Thou'lt deem, when thou hast done with earth,
These things of worth unspeakable,
Beside the gulf so black and drear,
The gulf of Fear, 'twixt Heaven and Hell.

A VISION OF HELL.

A Vision of Hell.

One fair morning of genial April, when the earth was green and pregnant, and Britain, like a paradise, was wearing splendid liveries, tokens of the smile of the summer sun, I was walking upon the bank of the Severn, in the midst of the sweet notes of the little songsters of the wood, who appeared to be striving to break through all the measures of music, whilst pouring forth praise to the Creator. I too occasionally raised my voice, and warbled with the feathered choir, though in a manner somewhat more restrained than that in which they sang; and occasionally read a portion of the book of the Practice of Godliness. Nevertheless, my former visions would not depart from my remembrance, but continually troubled me by coming across all other thoughts. And they persisted in doing so, until, by arguing the matter minutely with myself, I reflected that there is no vision but what comes from above, to warn one to be upon one's guard, and that consequently it was my duty to write mine down, that they might serve as a warning to others also. I therefore returned to my home, and whilst overwhelmed with melancholy. I was endeavouring to collect some of my frightful reminiscences, I happened to give a yawn over my paper, and this gave master Sleep an opportunity to glide upon the top of me. Scarcely had Sleep closed my senses, when, behold! a glorious apparition came towards me, in the shape of a young man, tall and exceedingly beautiful; his garments were seven times more white than snow, his countenance was so lustrous that it rendered the very sun obscure, and his curling locks of gold parted in two lovely wreaths upon his head, in the form of a crown. "Come with me, mortal man," said he on coming up. "Who art thou, my lord?" said I. "I am," he replied, "the angel of the countries of the North, the guardian of Britain and its queen. I am one of the princes who are stationed beneath the throne of the Lamb, who receive commands for the protection of the gospel, against all its enemies in Hell and in Rome, in France and Constantinople, in Africa and in India, and wheresoever else they are devising artifices for its destruction. I am the angel who conducted thee below to castle Belial, and who showed thee the vanity and madness of the whole world, the city of Destruction, and the excellence of the city of Emmanuel, and I am come once more by his command, to show thee other things, because thou art seeking to turn to account what thou hast seen already." "How, my lord," said I, "will your illustrious majesty, which superintends kings and kingdoms, condescend to associate with such a poor worm as myself?" "O," said he, "we respect more the virtue of a beggar than the grandeur of a sovereign. What if I be greater than all the kings of the earth, and higher than many of the countless potentates of heaven? As my wonderful master deigned to humble himself so inexpressibly as to wear one of your bodies, and to live among you, and to die for your salvation, how should I presume to be dissatisfied with my duty in serving you, and the vilest of the human race, since ye are so high in favour with my master? Come out, spirit, and free thyself from thy clay," said he, with his eyes directed upwards. And with that word, I could feel myself becoming extricated from every part of my body. No sooner was I free, than he snatched me up to the firmament of heaven, through the region of lightning and thunder, and all the glowing armories of the sky, innumerable degrees higher than I had been with him before, whence I could scarcely descry the earth, which looked no wider than a croft. After permitting me to rest a short space, he again lifted me up a million of miles, until I could see the sun far below us; we rushed through the milky way and past the Pleiades, and many other exceedingly large stars, till we caught a distant view of other worlds. At length, by dint of journeying, we reached the confines of the awful eternity, and were in sight of the two palaces of the mighty king Death, which stand one on the right hand and the other on the left, and are at a great distance from each other, as there is an immense void between them. I enquired whether we should go to see the right hand palace, because it did not appear to me to resemble the other which I had seen before. " You will probably see," he replied, "sometime, still more of the difference which is between the one palace and the other; but at present it is necessary for us to sail another course." Whereupon we turned away from the little world, and having arrived over the intervening gap, we let ourselves down to the country of Eternity, between the two palaces, into the horrible void; an enormous country it was, exceedingly deep and dark—without order and without inhabitants—now hot, now cold—sometimes silent, sometimes noisy, with the sound caused by cataracts of water tumbling upon the flames and extinguishing them: which cataracts, however, did not long continue, for presently might be seen a puff of fire bursting out and consuming the water. There was here no course, nor whole, nothing living, nothing shapely: but a giddy discord and an amazing darkness, which would have blinded me for ever, if my companion had not again displayed his heavenly garment of splendour. By the light which it cast I could see the country of Oblivion, and the edges of the wilds of Destruction in front, on the left hand; and on the right the lowest skirts apparently of the walls of Glory. "Behold the great gulf between Abraham and Dives," said my guide, "which is termed the place of Chaos. It is the region of the elements which God created first: it is the place wherein are the seeds of every living thing, from which the Almighty word made your world, and all that therein is—water, fire, air, earth, animals, fishes and creeping things, winged birds, and human bodies, but not your souls, for they are of an origin and generation higher and more exalted. Through the vast, frightful place of Chaos, we at length broke out to the left hand, and before travelling any distance there, where every thing was ever becoming more frightful, I could feel my heart at the top of my throat, and my hair standing like the prickles of the hedge-hog, even before seeing any thing; but when I *did* see—oh! spectacle too much for tongue to relate, or for the spirit of man to behold. I fainted. Oh, the amazing and monstrous abyss, opening in a horrible manner into the other world! Oh, the

continual crackling of the terrible flames, darting over the
sides of the accursed precipice, and the flashes of linked
lightning rending the black, thick smoke, which the unsightly
orifice was casting up! My dear companion, having brought
me to myself again, gave me some spiritual water to drink;
O how excellent it was in its taste and color! After drinking of the heavenly water, I could feel a wonderful strength
diffusing itself through me, bringing with it sense, heart, faith,
and various other heavenly virtues. By this time I had
approached with him unterrified to the edge of the steep,
enveloped in the veil, the flames parting on both sides and
avoiding us, not daring to come in contact with the inhabitants of the supreme abodes. Then from the summit of the
terrific precipice we darted down, like two stars falling from
the firmament of heaven, a thousand million of miles, over
many a brimstone crag, and many a furious, ugly cataract and
glowing precipice, every thing that we passed looking always
frowningly downward; yet every thing noxious avoided us,
except once, when having thrust my nose out of the veil, I
was struck by such a suffocating, strangling exhalation as
would have put an end to me, if my guide had not instantly
assisted me with the water of life. By the time that I had
recovered, I perceived that we had arrived at a kind of standing place; for in all this loathsome chasm it was impossible
to obtain any rest before, owing to the steepness and slipperi-
ness of its sides. There my guide permitted me to take some
further rest; and during this respite, it happened that the
thunders and the hoarse whirlwinds became silent for a little
while, and in spite of the din of the raging cataracts, I heard
from afar a sound louder than the whole—a sound of horrible
harsh voices, of shouting, bellowing, and strong groans,

swearing, cursing, and blaspheming, till I would have con-
sented to part with mine ears, that I might not hear. Ere
we moved a foot farther, we could hear a terrible tumbling
sound, and if we had not suddenly slipped aside, hundreds of
unfortunate men would have fallen upon us, who were coming
headlong, in excessive hurry, to take possession of their bad
purchase, with a host of devils driving them. "O, sir," said
one devil, "take it easy, lest you should ruffle your curling
locks. Madam, do you wish for an easy cushion? I am
afraid that you will be out of all order by the time you come
to your conch," said he to another.

The strangers were exceedingly averse to going forward,
insisting that they were out of their road; but notwithstanding all they could say, go they did, and we behind them, to a
black flood of great magnitude, and through it they went, and
we across it; my companion holding the celestial water
continually to my nostrils, to strengthen me against the
stench of the river, and against the time when I should see
some of the inhabitants of the place, for hitherto I had not
beheld so much as one devil, though I had heard the voices of
many. "Pray, my lord," said I, "what is the name of this
putrid river?" "The river of the Fiend," said he, "in which
all his subjects are bathed, in order that they may be rendered
fit for the country. For this accursed water changes their
countenance, and washes away from them every relic of goodness, every semblance of hope and of comfort." And, indeed,
on gazing upon the host after it had come through, I could
distinguish no difference in deformity between the devils and
the damned. Some of the latter would fain have sculked at the
bottom of the river, and have lain there to all eternity, in a
state of strangulation, lest they should get a worse bed farther

on; but here the proverb was verified, that "he must needs run whom the Devil drives," for with the devils behind, the damned were compelled to go forward unto the beach, to their eternal damnation; where I at the first glance saw more pains and torments than the heart of man can imagine or the tongue relate: a single one of which was sufficient to make the hair stand erect, the blood to freeze, the flesh to melt, the bones to drop from their places—yea, the spirit to faint. What is empaling or sawing men alive, tearing off the flesh piecemeal with iron pincers, or broiling the flesh with candles, collop fashion, or squeezing heads flat in a vice, and all the most shocking devices which ever were upon earth, compared with one of these? Mere pastime! Here were a hundred thousand shoutings, hoarse sighs, and strong groans; yonder a boisterous wailing and horrible outcry answering them, and the howling of a dog is sweet, delicious music, when compared with these sounds. When we had proceeded a little way onward from the accursed beach, towards the wild place of Damnation, I perceived, by their own light, innumerable men and women here and there; and devils without number and without rest, incessantly employing their strength in tormenting. Yes, there they were, devils and damned, the devils roaring with their own torments, and making the damned roar, by means of the torments which they inflicted upon them. I paid particular observation to the corner which was nearest me. There I beheld the devils with pitch-forks, tossing the damned up into the air, that they might fall headlong on poisoned hatchels or barbed pikes, there to wriggle their bowels out. After a time the wretches would crawl in multitudes, one upon another, to the top of one of the burning crags, there to be broiled like mutton; from there

they would be snatched afar, to the top of one of the mountains of eternal frost and snow, where they would be allowed
to shiver for a time; thence they would be precipitated into
a loathsome pool of boiling brimstone, to wallow there in
conflagration, smoke, and the suffocation of horrible stench;
from the pool they would be driven to the marsh of Hell, that
they might embrace and be embraced by its reptiles, many
times worse than serpents and vipers; after allowing them
half an hour's dalliance with these creatures, the devils would
seize a bundle of rods of steel, fiery hot from the furnace, and
would scourge them till their howlings, caused by the horrible
inexpressible pain which they endured, would fill the vast
abode of darkness, and when the fiends deemed that they had
scourged them enough, they would take hot irons and sear
their bloody wounds.

There was here no fainting, nor swooning to evade a
moment of suffering, but a continual strength to suffer and to
feel, though you would have imagined after one horrible cry,
that it would be utterly impossible there should be strength
remaining to give another cry so frightfully loud; the damned never lowered their key, and the devils kept replying,
"behold your welcome for ever and ever." And it almost
seemed that the sauciness and bitterness of the devils, in
jeering and mocking their victims, were worse to bear than
the pain itself. What was worst of all, their conscience was
at present utterly aroused, and was tearing them worse than a
thousand of the infernal lions. We proceeded farther and farther downward, and the farther we proceeded, the more horrible
was the work which was going on; the first place we came to
in our progress was a frightful prison, in which were many
human beings under the scourge of the devils, shrieking most

shockingly. "What place is this?" said I. "That," said the angel, "is the couch of those who cry 'woe is me that I did not—!' Hark to them for a moment!" "Woe is me that I did not purify myself in time from every kind of sin!" says one. "Woe is me that I did not believe and repent before coming here!" says the other.

Next to the cell of too late repentance, and of debate after judgment had been passed, was the prison of the procrastinators, who would be every time promising amendment, without ever fulfilling their promise. "When this business is over," says one, "I will turn over another leaf." "When this obstacle is removed, I will become a new man yet," says the other. But when the obstacle is removed, they are not a bit the nearer to reformation, for some other obstacle is always found to prevent them from moving towards the gate of Righteousness, and if they do sometimes move a little, they are sure to turn back. Next to this was the prison of vain confidence, full of those who, on being commanded to abstain from their luxuriousness, drunkenness, or avarice, would say, "God is merciful, and better than his word, and will not damn his creature for ever for so small a matter." But here they were yelping forth blasphemy, and asking where is that mercy, which was boasted to be immeasurable. "Peace, hell-dogs," at length said a great lobster of a devil who was hearing them, "peace! would you have mercy without doing any thing to obtain it? Would you have the Truth render his word false, for the sake of obtaining the company of such filthy dross as you? Too much mercy has been shown to you already. You were given a Saviour, a comforter, and the apostles, with books, sermons, and good examples, and will you never cease to deafen us with bawling about mercy, where mercy has never been?" On going out from this fiery gulf, I could hear one puffing and shouting terribly, "I knew no better, nothing was ever expended in teaching me my duty, and I could never find time to read or pray, because I was obliged to earn bread for myself and my poor family." "Aye," said a little crooked devil who stood by, "and did you never find time to tell pleasant stories?—no leisure for self vaunting, during long winter evenings when I was in the chimney corner? Now, why did you not devote some of that time to learning to read and pray? Who on Sundays used to come with me to the tavern, instead of going with the parson to church? Who devoted many a Sunday afternoon to vain prating about worldly things, or to sleep, instead of meditation and prayer? And have ye merely acted according to your knowledge and your opportunities? Peace, sirrah, with your lying nonsense!" "O thou blood of a mad dog!" said the lost man, "it is not long since you were whispering something very different into my ear, if you had said that the other day, I should scarcely have come here." "O," said the devil, "we do not mind telling you the bitter truth here, since we need not fear that you will go back to tell tales."

Below this cell I saw a kind of vast pit, and in it what looked like an infinite quantity of loathsome ordure, burning with a green flame, and on drawing near, I was aware, from the horrid howling that proceeded from it, that it was composed of men piled one upon another, the horrible flames crackling meanwhile through them. "This hollow said the angel, "is the couch of those who say after committing some great sin, 'pooh! I am not the first, I have plenty of companions;' and thus you see, they *do* get plenty of companions, to verify their words and to increase their agony." Opposite to this horrible place was a large cellar, where I could see men twisted, as tow is twisted, or hemp is spun. "Pray," said I, "who are these?" "Panegyrists," said he, "and out of sheer mockery to them, the devils are trying whether it is possible to twist them as flexibly as they twisted their own discourse." A little way below that cell, I could but just descry a sort of prison-pool, very dark, and in it things which had been men, having faces like the heads of wolf-dogs, and up to their jaws in bog, barking blasphemy and lies most furiously, as long as they could get their sting above the mud. At this moment a troop of devils happening to pass by, some of these creatures contrived to bite in the heels, ten or twelve of the devils who had brought them thither. "Woe and destruction to you hell-dogs!" said one of the devils who had been bit, "you shall pay for this;" and forthwith commenced beating the bog, till the wretches were drowned in the stinking abysses. "Who," he then added, "have deserved hell better than you, who have been hunting up and devising gossip, and buzzing lies about from house to house, in order that you might laugh, after having set a whole country at loggerheads. What more could one of ourselves have done?" "That," said the angel, "is the bed of the tale-bearers, the slanderers, and the whisperers, and of all other envious curs, who are continually wounding people behind their backs with their hands or their tongues."

From here we passed to a vast dungeon, by far the filthiest that I had seen yet, and the most replete with toads, adders, and stench. "This," said my guide, "is the place of the men who expect to get to heaven because they have no ill intentions, that is, for being neither good nor bad." Next to this pool of ill savour, I beheld a place where a vast crowd were sitting, and without any thing visible to torment them, groaning more piteously than any that I had hitherto heard in Hell. "Mercy upon us," said I, "what causes these people to complain more than the rest, when they have neither torture nor devil near them?" "O," said the angel, "the less torment they have without, the more they have within. These are refractory heretics, atheists, antichristians, worldly-wise ones, abjurers of the faith, persecutors of the church, and an infinity of such like wretches, who are abandoned entirely to the punishment of conscience, more tormenting than flame or devil, which domineers over them ceaselessly and without restraint. 'I will never permit myself any more,' says she, 'to be drowned in ale, nor to be blinded by bribes, nor deafened by music and company, nor lulled nor confounded by careless listlessness; for now I *will* be listened to, and never shall the clack of the hated truth cease in your ears.' Longing is ever raging within the wretch for the happiness which he has lost; memory is ever reproaching him by saying how easy it was to be obtained, and the understanding show-ing him the magnitude of his loss, and the certainty that nothing is now to be obtained, but indescribable gnawing for ever and ever. So with these three instruments—namely longing, memory, and understanding—conscience is tearing the lost one, in a manner far worse than all the devils in Hell could tear him with their claws."

On coming out of this wonderful nook I heard a confused talking, and after every word such a ghastly laughter, as if five hundred devils were casting their horns with laughing. On approaching to see the cause of such a rarity as laughter in Hell, I discovered that it was only got up to incense two honorable gentlemen, newly arrived, who were insisting on being shown respect suitable to their gentility. One of them was a round bodied squire, having with him a big roll of parchment—namely his map of pedigree—out of which he recited from which of the fifty tribes of North Wales he was sprung, and how many justices of the peace, and how many sheriffs his house had produced. "Come, come," said one of the devils, "we know the merits of the greater part of your ancestry. If you had been like your father or your great grandfather, we should not have ventured to come in contact with you; but you are only the heir of the pit of darkness, you dirty hell-dog! You are scarcely worthy of a night's lodging," added he, "and yet we'll grant you some nook, wherein to await the dawn;" and with that word the goblin with his pitchfork, gave him more than thirty tosses in the fiery air, until he at length cast him into an abyss out of sight. "That may do," said the other, "for a squire of half blood, but I hope you will behave better to a knight, who has had the honor of serving the king in person, and can name twelve earls and fifty baronets belonging to his ancient house." "If your ancestors and your ancient house be all that you can bring in your defence, you may go the same road as he," said one of the devils, "because we can scarcely remember one ancient house, of which some oppressor, murderer, or strong thief did not lay the foundation, and which he did not transmit to people as froward as himself, or to lazy drones, or drunken swine, to maintain whose extravagant magnificence, the vassals and the tenantry must be squeezed to death, whilst every handsome colt or pretty cow in the neighbourhood must be parted with for the pleasure of the mistress, and every lass or married woman, may consider herself fortunate, if she escape the pleasure of the master; the freeholders, meanwhile, being

either obliged to follow him like fawning hounds, rob themselves for his benefit, and sell their patrimonies at his pleasure,
or be subject to frowns and hatred, and be dragged into every
disagreeable and vexatious employment during their lives.

O these little great country folks," continued the devil,
"how genteelly they swear in order to obtain credit with their
mistresses, or with the shop-keepers; and when they have
decked themselves out, O how insolently they look upon many
of the middling officers of the church and state, and how
much worse on the common people! as if they were a species
of reptiles in comparison with themselves. Woe is me! is not
all blood of the same color? Did you not come all into the
world by the same way?" "But, nevertheless, with your
permission," said the knight, "there are some who are of
much purer birth than others." "Destruction take you!"
said the goblin, "there is not one carcass of you all better
than the rest; you are all polluted with radical sin from
Adam. But, sir," said he, "if your blood be better than
other blood, less scum will exude from you when boiling;
however, in order to be sure of its quality, it will be as well
to scorch you with fire as well as water." Thereupon a devil
in the shape of a chariot of fire received him, and the other in
mockery lifted him into it, and away he was hurried like
lightning. After a short time the angel caused me to look,
and I could see the wretched knight suffering a terrible
steeping in a frightful boiling furnace, in company with Cain,
Nimrod, Esau, Tarquin, Nero, Caligula, and the others who
were the founders of genealogies, and were the first to set up
arms of nobility.

A little farther on, my guide caused me to look through
the hollow of a rock, and there I beheld a number of coquettes

briskly at work, doing and repeating all their former follies
upon earth. Some were twisting their mouths, some were
pulling their front locks with irons, some were painting themselves, some patching their faces with sooty ointments, to
make the yellow look more fair; some quite mad at seeing
their visages, after all their pains in coloring and variegating,
more hideous than those of the very devils, were endeavouring
to break the mirrors, or were tearing off with their nails and
their teeth the whole artificial blush—the ointments, skin, and
flesh coming off all together. The cries which they uttered
occasionally were most dismal. "The curse of curses," would
one say, "on my father, for making me marry when a girl,
an old sapless stump, whose work in raising desires which he
could not gratify has driven me hither." "A thousand curses
on my parents," would another say, "for sending me to a
cloister to learn chastity; they would not have done worse in
sending me to a roundhead to learn generosity, or to a quaker
to learn manners, than to a papist to learn honor." "Destruction," said another. "seize my mother for her avaricious
pride in preventing my obtaining a husband when I wanted
one, and thus obliging me to purloin the thing I might have
honorably come by." "Hell, and double Hell to the lustful
wretch of a gentleman, who first began tempting me," would
the third say; "if he had not, betwixt fair and foul, broken
the hedge, I had not become a cell open to every body, nor
had I come to this cell of devils!" And then they fell
to tearing themselves again.

I was glad to quit such a pack of female dogs. But
before I had passed on many steps, I was surprised to see
another shoal of imprisoned wenches, twice more detestable
than they. Some had been changed into toads, some into

dragons, some into serpents who were swimming and hissing, glavering and butting in a fetid, stagnant pool, much larger than Llyn Tegid.‖ "In the name of wonder," said I, "what sort of creatures may these be?" "There are here," said he, "four sorts of wenches, all notoriously bad. First, there are procuresses, with some of the principal lasses of their respective bevies about them. Second, gossiping ladies with a swarm of their news-bearing hags. Third, bouncing madams, and a pack of sneaking curs on both sides of them, for no man, but for downright fear of them, would ever go nigh them. Fourth, scolds, become a hundred times more horrible than vipers, with their poisonous stings going creak, creak to all eternity."

"I had imagined that Lucifer had been a king of too much courtesy, to put a gentlewoman of my rank with such little petty she-devils as these," said one, something like a winged serpent, only that she was much more fierce. "O that he would send here, seven hundred of the worst devils in Hell in exchange for thee, thou poisonous hell-spawn!" said another ugly viper. "O! many thanks to you," said a gigantic devil who overheard them, "we set too much value on our place and merits, to condescend to become mates of yours; and though we are willing to admit that you are fully as competent to torment people as the best of us, we would, nevertheless, not yield up our duties to you." "And yet," said the angel softly, "Lucifer has another reason for keeping such a particular watch over these; he knows well, that if they should break out, they would turn all Hell topsy-turvy." From here we went, still going downward, to a place where I beheld a frightful den, in which was a horrible clamour, the like of

‖ Llyn Tegid, or the lake of Beauty, in the neighbourhood of Bala.

which I had never heard, for swearing, cursing, blaspheming, snarling, groaning, and crying. "Who is here?" said I. "This," said he, "is the den of the thieves. Here is a swarm of game-keepers, lawyers, stewards, and the old Judas in the midst of them; they have been excessively annoyed at seeing the tailors and weavers above them, in a more comfortable chamber." Almost before I could turn myself, there came a horse of a devil, bearing a physician and an apothecary, whom he cast down amongst the pedlars and the duffers, for selling bad, rotten ware; but they beginning to fume at being placed in such low company, one of the devils said, "stay, stay! you *do* deserve a different place," and cast them down amongst the conquerors and the murderers. There was a multitude shut up here, for playing with false dice and concealing cards; but before I could observe much, I heard, close by the door, a terrible rush and rustle, with a hie! hie! get on! ho! yo! hip! I turned to see what it was; but perceiving nothing but horned goblins, I enquired of my guide whether there were cuckolds amongst the devils? "No," said he, "they are in a particular cell. These are drovers who would fain escape to the place of the Sabbath-breakers, and are driven hither against their will." At that word, I looked, and perceived their polls full of the horns of sheep and cattle, and those who drove them, casting them down beneath the feet of the bloodiest robbers. "Crouch there," said one; "though you feared so much of old the thieves on London road, you were yourselves the very worst species of highwaymen, living upon the road and plundering, yes, and murdering poor families. O how many poor creatures did you not keep, with their hungry mouths open, in vain expectation of the money for the sale of the beasts, which they had intrusted to you; and you in the mean time in Ireland, or in the King's Bench laughing at them, or upon the road in the midst of your wine and harlots."

On quitting this den of furious heat, I got a sight of a lair, exceeding all the rest I had seen in Hell, but one, in frightful stinking filthiness, where was a herd of accursed drunken swine, disgorging and swallowing, swallowing and disgorging, continually and without rest, the most loathsome snivel. The next pit was the couch of gluttony, where Dives and his companions were upon their bellies, eating dirt and fire alternately, without any liquid ever. A cave or two lower there was an exceedingly spacious kitchen, in which some were in a state of roasting and boiling, others frying and burning in an oven half heated. "Behold the place of the merciless and the unfeeling," said the angel. I then turned a little to the left hand, where there was a cell more light than any one which I had yet seen in Hell, and enquired what place it was? "The abode of the infernal dragons," replied the angel, "who are hissing and snarling, rushing and preying upon one another every minute." I approached; and oh! the look which cannot be described was upon them, the whole light was but the living fire in their eyes. "These are the seed of Adam," said my guide, "morose wretches, and furious savage men; but, yonder," said he, "are some of the old seed of the great dragon Lucifer;" and verily, I could perceive not a whit more amiability in the one sort than in the other. In the next cellar were the misers, in a state of horrible agony, with their hearts cleaving to coffers of burning treasure, the rust whereof was ceaselessly cankering them, because those hearts had been ceaselessly bent upon getting money—O the consuming torment, worse than frenzy, that was now going on within them, with care and repentance. Below this there was a hanging ledge, where there were some apothecaries ground to dust, and stuffed into earthen pots amongst album græcum, dung of geese and swine, and many an old stinking ointment.

We were now journeying forward, continually descending, along the wilderness of Destruction, through innumerable torments, eternal and not to be described—from cell to cell, from cellar to cellar, and the last always surpassing the others in horror and ghastliness: at last we arrived at a vast porch, more cheerless than any thing we had seen before. It was a very spacious porch, and the pathway through it, which was frightfully steep, led to a kind of dusky nook of incredible ugliness and horror, and there the palace was.

At the upper end of the accursed court, among thousands of horrible objects, I could, by means of the radiance of my heavenly companion, perceive amidst the dreary darkness two feet of enormous magnitude, reaching to the roof of the whole infernal firmament. I enquired of my conductor what this horrible thing might be? "Patience," said he, "you shall obtain a more ample view of this monster as you return; but move forward now to see the royal palace."

Whilst we were proceeding down the porch of Horror, we heard a noise behind us, as of an immense number of people. Having turned aside to let them pass forward, we beheld four distinct bands, and soon discovered that the four princesses of the city of Destruction, were bringing their subjects as presents to their father. I recognised the princess Pride, not only by her being before the others, but also by her habit of stumbling every moment, for want of looking beneath her feet. She had with her a vast many kings, potentates, courtiers, gentlemen, and pompous people, many quakers, and innumerable females of every rank and degree.

The princess Lucre was next, with her silly, mean figure, bringing along with her very many of the money loving race—such as usurers, lawyers, extortioners, overseers, game-keepers, harlots, and some ecclesiastics also. Next to these was the amiable princess Pleasure and her daughter Folly, conducting their subjects—consisting of players at dice, cards, draughts, games of legerdemain, and of poets, musicians, tellers of old stories, drunkards, ladies of pleasure, debauchees, pretty fellows, with a thousand million of all kinds of baubles, to serve now as instruments of punishment for the lost fools. After these three had gone with their prisoners to the palace, to receive their judgment—behold Hypocrisy, the last of all, conducting a more numerous rout than any of the others, of all nations and ages, of town and country, gentle and simple, males and females. At the tail of the two-faced multitude we advanced till we came in sight of the palace, through many dragons and horned sprites, and warriors of Hell, the black wardens of the gloomy pandemonium, I all the time crouch-ing very carefully within my veil. We entered the frightful and awful edifice, every corner of which abounded with horror. The walls were immense rocks of glowing adamant, the pave-ment of an insufferably sharp flint, the roof of burning steel, meeting like an arch of greenish-blue and dusky-red flames, and in its size and its heat, resembling an immense vaulted baking oven.

Opposite to the door, on a flaming throne, the Arch-Fiend was seated, his principal lost angels on both sides of him, on thrones of fire terrible to behold—sitting according to their former rank in the regions of light, when they were amiable messengers. It would only be in vain to endeavour to relate how obscene and horrible they were; and the longer I looked at any one of them, seven times more hideous he appeared. In the midst, above the head of Lucifer, was a vast fist, holding a very frightful bolt. The princesses, after making their obeisance, returned to the world to their charges, without making any stay. As soon as they had departed, a gigantic, wide-mouthed devil, by command of the king, uttered a shout louder than a hundred discharges of artillery, as loud if possible as the last trumpet, for the purpose of summoning the infernal parliament. And lo! the rabble of Hell instantly filled the palace and the porch in every shape, after the image and similitude of the principal sin, which each delighted to thrust upon mankind. After commanding silence, Lucifer, with his look directed to the potentates nearest to him, began to speak, very graciously, in the following manner:—

"Ye potentates of Hell! princes of the black abodes of Despair! Though by our confederacy we have lost possession of those thrones, from which we once shone resplendent through the higher regions; our confederacy was, nevertheless, a glorious one, as we aimed at nothing less than the whole. And we have not lost the whole either; for lo! the extensive and profound regions, to the extremest wilds of vast Destruction, are yet beneath our sway. It is true we reign in horrible agony; but spirits of our eminence prefer ruling in torment to serving in ease. And besides this, we are on the eve of obtaining another world, more than three parts of the earth having been beneath my banner for a long time.

"And although the Almighty Enemy, sent his own son to die for the beings of that world; yet I, by my baubles,

obtain ten souls, for every one which he obtains by his
crucified son. And although I have not been able to reach
him, who sits in the high places and discharges the invincible
thunderbolts, yet revenge of some kind is sweet. Let us
complete the destruction of the remnant of human beings,
still in the favour of our destroyer. I remember the time,
when you caused them to be burnt by multitudes and cities,
and even the whole race of the earth, by means of the flood,
to be swept down to us in the fire. But at present, though
your strength and your natural cruelty are not a whit dimin-
ished, yet you are become in some degree inactive; if that
had not been the case, we might long since have destroyed
the few who are godly, and have caused the earth to be united
with this our vast empire. But know, ye black ministers of
my displeasure, that unless ye be more resolute and more
diligent, and make the most of the short time which yet
remains to you for doing evil, ye shall experience the weight
of my anger, in torments new and strange to the oldest of
you. This I swear by the deepest Hell, and the vast, eternal
pit of Darkness." And, thereupon, he frowned, till the palace
became seven times more gloomy than before.

Moloch now arose, one of the infernal potentates, and
after making his obeisance to the king, he said, "O emperor
of the Air! mighty ruler of Darkness! no one ever doubted
my propensity to malice and cruelty; the sufferings of others
have been, and still are, my supreme delight. It is as capital
sport to me, to hear the shrieks of infants perishing in the fire
as of old, when thousands of sucklings were sacrificed to me
outside of Jerusalem. When was I ever slack at my work?
Since the return of the crucified Enemy to the supreme abodes,
I have employed myself in slaying and burning his subjects.

I did all I could, to destroy the Christians from the face of the earth, during the reigns of ten emperors; and many an awful butchery I have made of them in modern times, both in Paris and England, to say nothing of other places: but what are we the nearer to our object for all this? The One above has caused the tree to grow, after its branches have been severed; and all our efforts, are nothing better than showing one's teeth, without the power of biting." "Pshaw!" said Lucifer, "a fig for such heartless legions as ye. I will no longer rely upon you! I will do the work myself, and the glory thereof I will share with no one. I will go to the earth in my own kingly person, and will swallow up the whole; not one man, henceforth, shall be found on the earth to adore the Almighty." Thereupon he gave a furious bound, attempting to set off, in a firmament of living fire; but, behold! the fist above his head shook the terrific bolt till he trembled in the midst of his frenzy, and before he could move far, an invisible hand lugged the old fox back by his chain, in spite of his teeth. Whereupon he became seven times more frantic; his eyes were more terrible than lightnings, black thick smoke burst from his nostrils, and dark green flames from his mouth and entrails: he gnawed his chain in his agony, and hissed forth direful blasphemy, and the most frightful curses.

But perceiving how vain it was to seek to break loose, or to struggle with the Almighty, he returned to his place and proceeded with his discourse somewhat more calmly, but with ten times more malice. "The Omnipotent Thunderer has vanquished me, and he alone could have done so. To him I submit. Against him all my fury is in vain; I will, therefore, direct it against nearer and lower objects, and pour it in showers upon those who are yet under my banner, and within the reach of my chain. Arise, ye ministers of Destruction! rulers of the unquenchable fire! and as my wrath and my venom flow forth and my malice boileth out, do ye assiduously spread the whole tide amongst the damned, particularly the Christians. Urge the instruments of torture to the utmost —devise as many more as you can—double the fire and the boiling, until the very cauldrons be overturned; and when they are in the most extreme, inexpressible torture, mock, deride, and upbraid them; and when your whole stock of irony and bitterness is expended, hasten to me, and you shall obtain more."

There had been for some time a comparative silence in Hell, and the more cruel tortures had been suspended; but how the stillness which Lucifer had caused was broken, when the ghastly butchers rushed like wild hungry bears upon their prisoners. O then there arose an oh! oh! oh! a wail, and universal howling, more loud than the sound of cataracts, or the tumult of an earthquake, so that Hell became seven times more frightful. I should have swooned if my dear companion had not rendered me assistance. "Take now," said he, "plenty of the water, that you may obtain strength to see things yet more horrible than these." But scarcely had these words proceeded from his mouth, when, lo! the celestial Justice, who sits above the precipice keeping the gate of Hell, came scourging three men with a rod of fiery scorpions. "Ha! ha!" said Lucifer, "here are three right reverend gentlemen, whom Justice himself has deigned to conduct to my kingdom." "Oh! woe is me," said one of the three, "who asked him to trouble himself?" "Be it known," said Justice, with a glance which made the devils tremble till they knocked one against another, "that it is the will of the Great Creator,

that I should myself bring these three accursed murderers to
their home. Sirrah," said he to one of the devils, "unbolt
for me the prison of the murderers, where are Cain and Nero,
Bonner, Bradshaw, Ignatius, and innumerable others of a
similar description." "Alas, alas! we never killed any body,"
said one of the prisoners. "No, because you did not get
time, and because you were prevented," said Justice. When
the den was opened, there came out such a horrible puff of
bloody flame, and such a yell as if a thousand dragons were
giving their last gasp in their death agony. Into this den
Justice hurled his prisoners;* and on his way back he breathed
obliquely, such a tempest of fiery whirlwinds upon the Arch
Fiend and all his potentates, as he passed by them, that
Lucifer, Beelzebub, Satan, Moloch, Abaddon, Asmodeus.
Dagon, Apollyon, Belphegor, Mephistophiles, and all the
other principal demons were whisked away, and tumbled
headlong into a kind of gulf, which was opening and closing
in the midst of the palace, and whose aspect was more
horrible, and whose steam was more frightful than the aspect
and vapour of any gulf which I had previously seen. Before I
could enquire of the angel as to what it was, he said, "that
is a hole which leads to another vast world." "Pray," said
I, "what is the name of that world?" "It is called," said he.
"Unknown, or extremest Hell, the habitation of the devils.
and the place to which they are at present gone. The vast
wilderness, over part of which you have come, is called the
country of Despair, a place intended for the lost until the
Day of Judgment, when it will fall into extremest, bottomless
Hell, and the two will become one. When that has happened

* The reader is left to guess what description of people these prisoners
were. They were probably violent fifth monarchy preachers.

one of ourselves will come and close the gate of the whole region of horror upon the devils and the damned, which gate shall never, to all eternity, be opened for them. In the meantime, however, permission is given to the devils to come to these cooler regions, in order to torment the lost souls. Yea, they often obtain permission to go even into the air, and about the earth, to tempt men to the destructive paths, which lead to this dismal prison, from which there is no escape." In the midst of this history, and whilst I was in great surprise at seeing the mouth of Unknown, so much surpassing in horror the jaws of upper Hell, I could hear a prodigious noise of arms, and loud discharges from one side, answered by what seemed to be hoarse thunders from the other; the rocks of Death, meanwhile, rebellowing the tumult.

"That is the sound of war," said I. "Is there war then in Hell?" "There is," said the angel; "and it is impossible that there should not be here continual war." Whilst we were moving out, to see what was the matter, I beheld the mouth of Unknown opening, and casting up thousands of candles, burning with a frightful green flame. These were Lucifer and his potentates, who had contrived to subdue the tempest. But when the Arch Fiend heard the noise of war, he became more pale than Death, and began to call and gather together bands of his old experienced soldiers to quell the tumult. At this moment he stumbled against a little puppy of an imp, who had escaped between the feet of the combatants. "What is the matter?" said the king. "Such a matter as will endanger your crown, unless you look to yourself," said the imp. Close behind him came another fiendish courier, bawling hoarsely, "you are plotting disquiet for others, look now to your own repose. Yonder are the

Turks, the Papists, and the bloody-handed Roundheads, in three bands, filling all the plains of the dark abodes, committing terrible outrages, and turning every thing topsy-turvy." "How came they out?" said the Arch Fiend, looking worse than Demigorgon. "The Papists," said the messenger, "broke out of their Purgatory, I do not know how; and then on account of an old grudge, they went to attack the back gate of the Paradise of Mahomet, and let all the Turks out of their prison; and afterwards, in the hubbub, the seed of Cromwell found some means to break out of their cells." Then Lucifer turned about and looked under his throne, where were all the lost kings, and caused Cromwell to be kept close in his kennel; and likewise all the emperors of the Turks, under watch and ward. He then hastened with his legions along the black wilds of Darkness, each obtaining light from the fire which was incessantly tormenting his body. Guided by the horrid uproar, the fiends advanced courageously towards the combatants; then silence was enjoined in the name of the king, and Lucifer enquired, "what is the cause of this disturbance in my kingdom?" "Please, your infernal majesty," said Mahomet, "a dispute arose between me and pope Leo, as to whether my Koran or the creed of Rome, had rendered you most service; and whilst we were at it, a pack of Roundheads broke their prison and put in their oar; asserting that their league and covenant, deserved more respect at your hands than either. Thus from disputing we have come to blows, and from words to arms. But at present, as your majesty has returned from Unknown, I will refer the matter to yourself." "Stay, we shall not let you escape thus!" said pope Julius; and to it again they went, tooth and nail, in the most furious manner, till the strokes were like an earthquake. O you should have seen the three armies of the damned, tearing one another to pieces, over the expanse of the burning plains; and each individual body that was rent to pieces, becoming joined again serpent fashion. At last Lucifer caused his old soldiers, the champions of Hell, to pull them from each other, and it was no easy matter to do so.

When the tumult was hushed, pope Clement began to speak. "O emperor of Horrors! as no throne has ever performed more faithful and universal service to the infernal crown, over a great part of the world, for eleven hundred years, than the papal chair, I hope you will not suffer any one to contend with us for your favour." "Well," said a Scott of Cromwell's army, "though the Koran has done great service for eight hundred years, and the superstition of the Pope for a much longer period, yet has the covenant done more since it came out, than the other two have ever done. Moreover it is notorious that, whilst the votaries of those two are every day rapidly diminishing, the followers of the covenant are increasing in numbers, over the whole face of the world, and particularly in the island of your enemies Britain, whose capital, London, the most noble city under the sun, abounds with them." "Pshaw, pshaw!" said Lucifer, "if I am rightly informed, the covenant itself is under a cloud, and you are no longer what you were. And now I have one thing to tell the whole of you—which is, that, whatever ye may do in other kingdoms, I will not permit you to trouble mine. Therefore rest peaceably, under penalty of worse torments corporeal and spiritual." At those words many of the devils dropped their tails between their hoofs, and all the damned sneaked away to their holes, for fear of a change for the worse.

After causing the whole of them to be locked up in their prisons, and the careless wardens to be deprived of their office, for having permitted them to break out, Lucifer and his counsellors returned to the palace, and sat down again, according to their rank, upon their fiery thrones. After silence had been called and the place cleared, a huge, wry-shouldered devil, placed a back-load of fresh prisoners before the bar. "Is this the road to Paradise," said one, (for they all pretended not to know where they were.) "Or if this be Purgatory," said another, "we have with us an authority, under the hand of the Pope, to go straight to Paradise without tarrying any where a minute. Therefore show us the way, or, by the Pope's toe, we will cause him to punish you." Ha! ha! ha!—ho! ho! ho! said eight hundred devils; and Lucifer himself, parted his jaws half a yard in a kind of bitter laugh. The others were confounded at this; but one said, "well, if we have lost our way in the darkness, we would pay any one who would guide us." "Ha! ha!" said Lucifer, "you will pay the last farthing before ye go." Thereupon each fell to searching for his money, but found, to his sorrow, that he had left his breeches behind him. Quoth the Arch Fiend, "you left Paradise on the left hand, above the lofty mountains; and, notwithstanding, it was so easy to come down here, it is next to impossible to go back, owing to the nature of the country, through which the road back lies. For it is a country abounding with mountains of burning iron, immense dismal crags, sheets of eternal ice, and roaring, headlong cataracts; a country, in short, far too difficult for you to travel, unless indeed you have talons of the true devilish length. Come, come," said he to his myrmidons, "take these blockheads to our paradise, to their companions."

At this moment I could hear the voice of some people who were coming, swearing and cursing in a frightful manner. "O the Devil! the blood of the Devil! a hundred thousand devils! a thousand million devils take me if I will go farther!" but, nevertheless, they were cast slap down before the judge. "Here you have," said the carrier, "a load of as good fire wood as the best in Hell." "What are they?" said Lucifer. "Masters of the genteel art of cursing and swearing," replied the devil; "men who understand the language of Hell, quite as well as ourselves." "You lie in your mouth, by the Devil!" said one of them. "Sirrah! do you take my name in vain?" said the Arch Fiend. "Quick! and hang them by their tongues to the burning precipice yonder, and if they call for the Devil, be ready to serve them: yea, if they call for a thousand, let them be satisfied." When these were gone, lo! a giant of a devil vociferated to have the bar cleared, and flung down a man whom he bore. "What have you brought there?" said Lucifer. "A tavern-keeper," replied the other. "What," said the king, "*one* tavern-keeper! Why they are in the habit of coming to the tune of five or six thousand. Have you not been out, sirrah, for ten years, and yet you bring us but one? and he one who has done us much more service in the world than yourself, you lazy, stinking dog!" "You are too ready to condemn me, before listening to me," he replied. "This fellow only was given to my charge, and, behold! I am clear of him. But still I have sent to you from his house, many a worthless chap, after guzzling down the maintenance of his family; many a dicer and card-player; many a genteel swearer; many a pleasant, good kind of belly god; and many a careless servant." "Well," said the Arch Fiend, "though the tavern-keeper has merited to be amongst the flatterers below us, take him at present to his brethren, in the cell of the liquid murderers; to the thousands of apothecaries and poisoners, who are there for making drink to kill their customers—boil him well for not having brewed better ale." "With your permission," said the tavern-keeper shivering, "I have deserved no such treatment. Must not every trade live?" "And could you not live," said the Fiend, "without encouraging dissipation and gaming, uncleanness, drunkenness, oaths, quarrels, slander and lies? and would you, hell-hound, live at present better than ourselves! Pray what evil have we here that you had not at home, the punishment solely excepted? And having told you this bitter truth, I will add, that the infernal heat and cold were not unknown to you either.

"Did you not see sparks of our fire in the tongues of the swearers and of the scolds, when seeking to get their husbands home? Was there not plenty of the unquenchable fire in the mouth of the drunkard, and in the eyes of the brawler? And could you not perceive something of the infernal cold in the lovingness of the spendthrift, and in your own civility to your customers, whilst any thing remained with them—in the drollery of the buffoons, in the praise of the envious and the backbiter, in the promises of the wanton, or in the shanks of the good companions freezing beneath your tables? Art thou unacquainted with Hell, when the house thou didst keep was Hell? Go, hell-dog, to thy punishment."

At this moment appeared ten devils with their burdens, which they cast upon the fiery floor, puffing terribly. "What have you there?" said Lucifer. "We have brought," said one of the fiendish carriers, "five things which were called kings the day before yesterday." (I looked attentively and beheld in one of them old Louis of France.) "Fling them here," said the king; whereupon they were flung to the other crowned heads, under the feet of Lucifer.

It was not long before I heard the sound of a brazen trumpet, and a crying of room! room! room! After waiting a little time, what should be coming but a drove of sessions folk, the devils carrying six lumps of justices and a thousand of their fry—consisting of lawyers, attornies, clerks, recorders, bailiffs, catchpoles, and pettifoggers of the courts. I was surprised that none of them attempted to cross-question; but they perceived that the matter was gone against them too far, and so, not one of these learned disputers opened his mouth; only a pettifogger of the courts said, that he would lay a plaint of false imprisonment against Lucifer. "You shall now have cause enough to complain," said the Fiend, "and yet never have an opportunity of seeing a court with your eyes." Then, putting on his red cap, Lucifer, with an arrogant, insufferable look, said, "take the justices to the dungeon of Pontius Pilate and Mr. Bradshaw, who condemned king Charles. Parch the lawyers in company with the murderers of Sir Edmund Bury Godfrey,† and their double-tongued brethren, who dispute with one another, for no other purpose than to be the ruin of any one who comes betwixt them. Let them greet that provident lawyer—for they will find him here—who offered on his death bed a thousand pounds for a clear conscience. Let them greet him, and ask, whether he is now willing to give any thing more. Roast them with their own parchment and papers; hang the petti-foggers above them, with their nostrils downwards, in the

† An active London Magistrate, treacherously murdered by a gang of papist conspirators in the reign of Charles the Second.

roasting chimneys, to receive the smoke, and to see whether they can get their belly-full of law. As for the recorders, let them be cast among the forestallers, who detain the corn or buy it up and mix it, and then sell the unsound for double the price of the pure corn; just as the former demand double the fees for *wrong*, which were formerly given for *right*. As for the catchpoles, leave them at liberty to hunt vermin; or send them to the world, among the dingles and brakes, to seize the debtors of the infernal crown—for what devil among you will do the work better than they?" At this moment twenty devils with packs on their shoulders, like Scotchmen, mounted before the throne of Despair, and what had they got, on enquiry, but gipsies. "Ho!" said Lucifer, "how did ye know the fortunes of others so well, without knowing that your own fortune was leading ye to this prison." But the gipsies said not a word in reply, being confounded at beholding faces here more ugly than their own. "Hurl them into our deepest dungeon," said Lucifer, to the fiends, "and don't starve them; we have here neither cats nor rush-lights to give them, but let them have a toad between them, every ten thousand years, provided they are quiet, and do not deafen us with their gibberish and clibberty clabber." Next to these there came, I should imagine, about thirty husbandmen. Every one was surprised to see so many of them, people of their honest calling seldom coming to Hell; but they were not from the same neighbourhood, nor for the same offences. Some were for raising the markets; many for refusing to pay tithes, and cheating the minister of his rights; others for leaving their work, to follow gentry a hunting, and breaking their legs in endeavouring to leap with them; some for working on Sundays; some for carrying their sheep and cattle, in their heads to church, instead of musing on the Word; others for roguish bargains. When Lucifer began to question them, oh! they were all as pure as gold; none was aware of having committed any thing which deserved such a lot. You will not believe what a crafty excuse every one had to conceal his fault, notwithstanding he was in Hell on account of it, and this was only done out of malice, to thwart Lucifer, and to endeavour to make the righteous Judge, who had damned them appear unjust. But you would have been yet more surprised at the dexterity with which the Arch Fiend laid bare their crimes, and answered their vain excuses home. But when these were receiving the last infernal sentence, there came forty scholars before the court, mounted on capering devils, more ugly, if possible, than Lucifer himself. And when the scholars heard the husbandmen arguing, they began to excuse themselves the more confidently. But, oh! how ready the old Serpent was at answering them too, notwithstanding their craft, and their learning.

But as it was my fortune to hear similar disputations at another tribunal, I will there give the history of the whole, in one mass; and will at present relate to you what I next saw. Scarcely had Lucifer uttered judgment upon these people, and sent them, for the cool impertinence of their reasons, to the vast sheet, in the country of the eternal ice, the teeth of the wretches beginning to chatter before they saw their prison, when Hell began once more, to resound awfully with terrible blows, harsh blustering thunders, and every sound of war. I could see Lucifer turn black, and become like a statue: at this moment, in rushed a little crooked, horned devil, panting and shivering. "What is the matter?" said Lucifer. "The most perilous to you of all matters since Hell has been Hell," said the imp; "all the extremes of the kingdom of Darkness, have broken out against you, and against one another; particularly those who had any old field in common. They are now at it, tooth and nail, so that it is impossible to tear them from each other.

"The soldiers are at loggerheads with the physicians, for carrying on their trade of slaughter; there is a swarm of usurers at loggerheads with the lawyers, for seeking to spoil their trade; the jurymen and the duffers are pummelling the gentlemen, for swearing and cursing without necessity; whereas, swearing and cursing formed part of their trade; the harlots, and their associates, and millions of other old friends and acquaintances, have fallen out, and are all in shatters.

"But worse than all, is the contest between the old misers and their own children, for dissipating their wealth and their money. 'Our property,' say the pigtails, 'cost us much pain, whilst we were upon the earth, and is causing us immense suffering *here* for ever, yet ye have flung it all away at ducks and drakes.' And the children, on the other hand, are cursing and tearing the old skin-flints, most furiously, charging their fathers with being the authors of their misery, by leaving them twenty times *too much*, to distract them with pride and dissipation; whereas, a *little*, with a blessing, might have made them happy in both their states of existence." "Well," said Lucifer, "enough! enough! we have more need of arms than words. Sirrah, this hubbub is owing to some great neglect; go back, and pry into every watch, and discover who has been neglectful; and what dangerous characters have been permitted to escape, for there are some evils abroad, that are not known." Away

he went, at the word, and in the meanwhile. Lucifer and his
potentates arose in terror, and exceeding consternation, and
caused the boldest bands of the black angels to be assembled.
When these were marshalled, he put himself at the head of
his own peculiar band, and marched forth to quell the insur-
rection, whilst the potentates went other ways with their
legions.

Before the royal troop had gone any great distance,
gleaming like the lightning of the black abodes, (and we
behind them,) behold the hubbub advanced to meet them.
"Silence, in the name of the king," said a fiendish herald.
There was no hearing; it was easier to tear the old crocodile
from his prey than one of these.

But when the old tried soldiers of Lucifer broke into the
midst of them, the buzzing, the butting, and the blows began
to slacken. "Silence, in the name of Lucifer," said the
hoarse cryer again. "What is the matter?" said the king;
"and who are these?" "There is nothing particularly the
matter," was the answer; "but the drovers, happening in the
general commotion to come in contact with the cuckolds, they
went mutually to butting. to try whose horns were hardest;
and this butting might have gone on for ever, if your horned
champions had not interfered." "Well," said Lucifer, "since
you are all so ready with your arms, turn along with me to
quell other rioters." But when it was buzzed about among
the other rebels, that Lucifer was coming with three horned
legions against them, each slunk away to his lair.

Thus Lucifer advanced without opposition, along the
wildernesses of Destruction, endeavouring to ascertain what
was the commencement of the disturbance, but could obtain
no information. After a little time, however, one of the spies

of the king returned, quite out of breath. "O most noble Lucifer!" said he, "prince Moloch has quieted part of the North, and has scattered thousands over the sheets of ice; but three or four terrible evils are still out on the wind." "Who are they?" said Lucifer. "*Slanderer*, and *Meddler*, and *Litigious Pettifogger*," said he, "have broken their prisons and are at liberty." "Then it would be no wonder," said the Arch Fiend, "if there should be yet more disturbance."

At this moment there came another, who had been on the look-out towards the South, with the information that the evil had begun to break out there; but that three had been taken, who had previously turned every thing topsy-turvy in the West, and these three were *Madam Bouncer*, *Contriver*, and *Coxcomb*. "Well," said Satan, who was standing next but one to Lucifer, "since I tempted Adam from his garden, I have never yet seen from his seed, so many evils out upon one piece of business.

"Bouncer, Coxcomb, and Contriver on the one side," he added, "and on the other Slanderer, Pettifogger, and Meddler are a compound, enough to make a thousand devils sweat their bowels out." "It is no wonder," said Lucifer, "that they are so detested by every body on earth, when they are able to cause us so much trouble here." A little farther on, a great bouncing lady struck against the king, as she was moving backwards. "Ho! my aunt of the breeches," said a hoarse devil, "good night to you." "Yes, your aunt, indeed! on what side pray?" said she, very wrathful, because she was not called madam.

"A pretty king are you, sir Lucifer," said she, "to keep such unmannerly blockheads; it is a sin that so large a kingdom should be under one so incompetent to govern them.

O that I were made deputy over it!" At this moment behold the *Coxcomb*, nodding his head in the dark. " Your servant, sir," he would say to one over his shoulder.—"I hope you are quite well," said he to another.—" Is there any service which I can render you," to a third, smiling conceitedly.—" Your beauty ravishes my heart," said he to the bouncing wench. "Oh! oh! away with this hell-dog." said she; whilst every one cried, "away with this new tormentor! Hell upon Hell is he!" "Bind him and her head to tail." said Lucifer.

After a little time, behold *Courts Comprised* held betwixt two devils. "O ho! angel of patience," said Lucifer, "are you come? Hold him fast on your peril," said he to the satellites. Before we had advanced far, there came the *Contriver* and the *Slanderer* bound betwixt forty devils, and whispering in each others ears. "O most mighty Lucifer!" said the *Contriver*, "I am exceedingly grieved to see so much disturbance in your dominions, but I will teach you a way to prevent such in future, if you will but grant me a hearing. You only need, under pretence of a general parliament, to summon all the damned to the glowing pandemonium, and then cause the devils to cast them headlong into the throat of *Unknown*, and the gulf to be closed over them, and then, I warrant you, they will give you no more trouble." "See," said Lucifer, frowning very horribly on the *Contriver*, "the universal Meddler is still behind." On returning again to the porch of the infernal palace, who should come with the fairest face imaginable to meet the king but the *Meddler*. "O my liege," said he, "I have a word for you." "Perhaps I have one or two for you," said the Fiend. "I have been," continued the Meddler, "over half *Destruction*, to observe how your affairs are standing. You have many officers in the East doing nothing at all; but sitting still instead of looking to the torments of their prisoners, or keeping guard over them, and this has been the cause of all this great disturbance. Besides," said he, "many of your devils, and your damned too, whom you dispatched to the world to tempt folks, are not returned, though their time is out; and others have arrived in a sculking manner, and not given an account of their errands."

Then Lucifer caused the herald to proclaim another parliament; and lo! before you could turn your hand, all the potentates and satellites were met together, to hold the infernal sessions again. The first thing which was done was to change the officers, and to cause a place to be made about the throat of Unknown, for the reception of the Coxcomb, the bouncing lady, and the rest; the two first were tied nose to nose, and the other rioters tail to tail. Then a law was promulgated, that whoever should henceforth neglect his duty, whether imp or lost man, should be cast there among them until the day of judgment. At these words you might see all the goblins—yea, Lucifer himself—tremble and look agitated. The next thing was to call some devils and some damned to reckoning, who had been sent to the world to hunt up recruits: the devils gave a very good account of themselves; but some of the damned were lame in their reckoning, and were sent to the hot school, where they were scourged with twisted fiery serpents, for not learning their lesson better.

"Hear my complaint," said a little informing devil. "Here is a pretty woman when trimmed out, who was sent up to the world, to hunt subjects for you by means of their hearts; and to whom did she offer herself, but to a hard-working labourer coming home late from his occupation, who instead of enjoying himself with her, went upon his knees to pray against the Devil and his angels: at another time, she went to a sick man." "Ha!" said Lucifer, "cast her to that lost useless wench, who loved of yore Einion ab Gwalchmai,‡ of Anglesey." "Stay," said the fair one, "this is but the first offence. It is not yet above a year, since the day when I breathed my last, and was damned to your accursed government." "She speaks true, O king of Torments! It is not yet a year by three weeks," said the devil who had brought her there. "Therefore," said she, "how would you have me so well versed as the damned, who have been here for three hundred, or out abroad depredating for five hundred years. If you desire from me better service, let me go into the world another time or two unchastised; and if I do not bring you twenty harlot-mongers, for every year that I am out, inflict upon me whatever punishment you please." But the verdict went against her, and she was condemned to punishment for a hundred long years, that she might remember better the second time.

At this moment, behold another devil pushing a fellow forward. "Here you have," said he, "a pretty dog of a messenger. As he was prowling about his old neighbourhood, above stairs, the other night, he saw a thief going to steal a stallion, and could not so much as help him to catch the horse without showing himself, frightening the thief so by his horrible appearance, that he took warning and became an honest man from that time." "With the permission of the court," said the fellow, "if the thief had got the gift from

‡ A celebrated Welsh poet, who flourished in the thirteenth century. A short account of him will be found in Owen's Cambrian Biography, page 107.

above to see me, could I help it? But at worst this is a single peccadillo," said he; "it is not above a hundred years since the day which terminated my mortal career, yet how many of my friends and neighbours have I not tempted hither after me, during that time? May I be in the deepest pit, if I have not as much inclination for the trade as the best of you; but now and then the craftiest will err." "Here," said Lucifer, "cast him to the school of the fairies, who are yet under the rod for their mischievous conduct of old, in strangling some people and threatening others; startling by such behaviour their neighbours from their heedlessness, upon whom the terror which they caused, had probably more effect than twenty sermons would have had."

Next appeared four catchpoles, an informer, and fifteen damned, hauling two *devils* forward. "See," said the informer, "lest you should lay the blame of all that is mismanaged on the seed of Adam, we bring you two of your old angels, who have spent their time above, quite as badly as the two preceding. Here is a fellow who has been making as great a fool of himself, as the Devil did at Shrewsbury the other day; who, in the midst of the interlude of Doctor Faustus, whilst some, according to the custom on such occasions, were committing adultery with their eyes, some with their hands, others making assignations for the same purpose, and doing various other things profitable to your kingdom, made his appearance to play his own part; by which blunder, he drove every one from taking his pleasure to praying. In like manner did this numskull act: for, whilst journeying over the world, on hearing two wenches talking of walking round the church at night, in order to see their sweethearts, he must needs show himself in the figure he wears at home, to the two fools, who on recovering their senses, which at first they lost from fright, solemnly abjured all frivolity for ever. There's a ninny-hammer for you! Instead of appearing like a devil, he ought to have divided himself and assumed the forms of two dirty, unlicked boors; for the girls would have imagined themselves bound to accept them, and then the filthy goblin might have lived as husband with the two female parties, without troubling a clergyman to perform the marriage.

"And here is another," said he, "who went the last dark night, to visit two young maidens in Wales, who were *turning the shift*; and instead of enticing the girls to wantonness in the figure of a handsome youth, he must needs go to one with a *hearse* to sober her; and to the other with the *sound of war* in an infernal whirlwind, to drive her farther from her senses than she was before, and there was no need for that. But this is not the whole, for after going into the last girl, he cast her down and tormented her furiously, so that her parents in horror, sent for some of our enemies the clergy, to pray over her and cast him out, which they did. Now, if he had been wise, instead of kicking up such a hubbub, he would have tempted her quietly to despair, and to make away with herself. On another time, wishing to gain some of the conventiclers, he went to preach to them, and revealed the secrets of your kingdom; thus, instead of hindering, assisting their salvation." At the word *salvation*, I could see some emitting living fire for madness. "Capital stories both, I won't deny," said the goblin; "but I hope that Lucifer will not permit one of Adam's race of dirt, to put himself on an equality with me who am an angel, of a species and descent far superior." "Ha!" said Lucifer, "he may be sure of his punishment. But, sirrah, answer to these accusations speedily and clearly, or by hopeless Destruction I will—" "I have brought hither," said the goblin, "many a soul since Satan was in the garden of Eden, and ought to know my trade better than this novice of an informer." "Blood of an infernal fire-brand!" said Lucifer, "did I not command you to answer speedily and clearly." "Do but hear me," said the sprite. As to preaching, by your own command I have been a hundred times *preaching*, and have forbidden people to follow several of the roads which lead to your territories, and yet silently, in the same breath, have led them hither safe enough, by some other vain paths; as I have done by preaching lately in Germany, and in one of the Faroe isles, and various other places.

"Thus through my preaching," he continued, "have come many of the *superstitions* of the papists, and the *old fables* first to the world, and the whole under the shape of some goodness. For who ever swallows the hook without some bait? who ever would believe a story if there were not some measure of *truth* mingled with the falsehood; or some semblance of *good* to shade the *evil?* Thus if I find an opportunity in preaching, to push in amongst a hundred correct and salutary counsels, one of my own, with this one I will do you, either through *contentiousness* or *superstition*, more advantage than all the rest of my counsels will do you harm." "Well," said Lucifer, "since you are of such utility in your pulpit, I order you for seven years, to take up your abode in the mouth of one of the barn-preachers, who will be sure to utter the first thing which comes to his tongue's end. Then you will find an opportunity to put in a word now and then, to your own purpose."

There were still many more devils and damned, who were twisting through one another like lightning, around the throne of Terrors, to give an account of what they had done, and again to receive commissions. But suddenly and unexpectedly, an order was given to all the messengers and the prisoners, to go out of the palace, every one to his hole, and to leave the king and his chief counsellors there alone. "Had we not best depart," said I to my companion, "lest they should find us?" "You need not fear," said the angel, "no unclean spirit will ever see through this veil." Thus we continued there invisible, to see what was the matter. Then Lucifer began to speak graciously to his counsellors, in this manner:—"O ye, the chief spiritual evils!—ye, who for subtlety are unequalled in Unknown, I request you in my need, to exert to the uttermost your malicious wiles. No one here is unaware, that Britain and the surrounding isles, constitute the kingdom most dangerous to my authority, and most abounding with my enemies; and what is a hundred times worse, there is at present there a queen, who does not offer to turn once hitherward, either by the road of Rome on the one hand, or the road of Geneva on the other. Notwithstanding, all the service which the Pope has rendered us there for a long time, and Oliver for some years past, how far are we from our object? what shall we do now? I am afraid that we shall lose there our ancient possession, and our market entirely, if we do not pave immediately some new way for its inhabitants to walk in, for they know all the old roads which lead hither too well. And, since yonder invincible fist shortens my chain, and prevents me from going myself to the earth, counsel me, I pray you, as to whom I shall make my deputy, to oppose yonder detestable queen, who is the deputy of our enemy." "O mighty emperor of Darkness!" said Cerberus, the devil of Tobacco, "make a deputy of me, from whom the crown of Britain derives the third part of its revenue. I will go and will send to you a hundred thousand of the souls of your enemies, through the hollow of a pipe." "Well, well," said Lucifer, "you have done me excellent service, by causing the proprietors of tobacco in India to be slaughtered, and those who take it to die of diseases, and sending many to vend it idly from house to house, and making others to steal in order to obtain it, and thousands to love it so far, that they cannot be a day without it in their right senses.

"Therefore go and do thy best; but, I tell thee, that thou art little better than nothing in the present exigency." Thereupon Cerberus sat down, and uprose Mammon, devil of Money, and with a morose sinister look said:—"I showed men the first mine from which they got money, and therefore, I am always extolled and worshipped more than God; men undergo for me trouble and danger, and place their whole mind, their delight, and their trust upon me: there is no one easy, because he has not obtained somewhat more of my favour, and the more they obtain the farther are they ever from rest, until at length by seeking *easy circumstances*, they arrive at the country of Eternal Torments. How many a crafty old miser have I not deluded hither, along paths more difficult than those which lead to the kingdom of Happiness? At fair or market, sessions or elections, or any other assemblage of people, who has more subjects? who has more power and authority than I? Cursing, swearing, fighting, litigating, plotting, deceiving, striking, hoarding, murdering and robbing, sabbath breaking and uncharitableness, all proceed from me;

and there is no other black mark, which stamps men as belonging to the fold of Lucifer, which I have not a hand in giving, on which account I am called 'the root of all evil.' Therefore if it seem good to your majesty, I will go." And having said that he sat down.

Then arose Apollyon. "I do not know," said he, "any thing that will bring the Britons hither, more certainly than what brought yourselves—that is *Pride:* if she ever plant her pole within them and inflate them, there is no reason to fear that they will stoop to lift the cross, or go through the narrow gate. I will go," said he, "with my daughter Pride, and will cause the Welsh, by gazing on the magnificence of the English, and the English, by imitating the frivolities of the French, to tumble into this place before they know where they are."

Next arose Asmodeus, devil of Wantonness. "You cannot but be aware," said he, "O most mighty sovereign of the Abyss! and you, ye princes of the country of Despair! how I have crammed the nooks of Hell through debauchery and lasciviousness. What need have I to speak of the time, when I kindled such a flame of lust in the whole world, that it was necessary to send the flood, to clear the earth of its inhabitants, and to sweep them to us in the unquenchable fire; or of Sodom and Gomorrah, fair and pleasant cities, whose people I burnt with wantonness, till their infernal lusts brought down a fiery shower, which drove them hither alive to burn to all eternity; or of the vast army of the Assyrians, which was slain all in one night on account of me? Sarah I disappointed of seven husbands; Solomon, the wisest of men, and many thousand other kings I blinded by means of women. Therefore," said he, "suffer me to go with my *sweet sin,* and I will kindle in Britain the sparks of Hell so universally, that it shall become one with this place of unextinguishable flame; for there is not much chance, that any one will return from following me, to lay hold of the paths of Life." And thereupon he sat down.

Then arose Belphegor, prince of *Sloth and Idleness.* "I am," said he, "the great prince of Listlessness and Laziness; great is my power on myriads of men of all ages and degrees. I am the still pool, where 'the root of all evil' is generated; where coagulate the dregs of all destructive corruption and filthiness. What would you be worth, Asmodeus; or you, ye other master spirits of evil, without me who keep the window open for you, without any watch, so that you may go into man by his eyes, by his ears, by his mouth, and by every other orifice which he has, whensoever you please. I will go, and will roll to you all the inhabitants of Britain over the precipice in their sleep."

Then arose Satan, the devil of *Deceit,* who sat next to Lucifer on his left hand, and after turning a frightful visage on the king,—"It is unnecessary for me," he said, "to declare my deeds to you, O lost archangel! or to you, black princes of Destruction! because it was I who struck the first blow which man ever received; and a mighty blow it was, causing him to remain *mortal,* from the beginning of the world to its end. Do you imagine that I, who despoiled the whole world, cannot at present give counsel which will serve for a paltry islet? And cannot I, who cheated *Eve* in *Paradise,* vanquish *Anne* in *Britain?* If no natural craft will avail, and continued experience for more than five thousand years, my counsel to you is, to dress up your daughter *Hypocrisy,* to deceive Britain and its queen; you have not a daughter in

the world, so useful to you as she; she has more extensive
authority and more numerous subjects, than all your other
daughters. Was it not through *her* that I cheated the first
woman? It was: and ever from that time she has remained
and increased exceedingly upon the earth. At present indeed,
the whole vast world is but one *Hypocrisy;* and if it were not
for the skill of Hypocrisy, how should any one of us do
business in any corner of the world? Because if people were
to see *sin* in its own *color,* and under its own *name,* who would
ever come in contact with it? The world would no more do
so, than it would embrace the Devil in his infernal shape
and garb. If Hypocrisy were not able to disguise her *name,*
and the *nature* of every *evil,* under the similitude of some
good, and were not able to give some evil nickname to all
goodness, no one would approach, and no one would covet evil
at all. Traverse the whole city of Destruction, and you will
see her in every corner. Go to the street of *Pride,* and enquire
for an *arrogant man,* or for a pennyworth of *coquetry,* mixed
up by Pride: 'woe's me,' says Hypocrisy, 'there is no such
thing here; nothing at all I assure you, in the whole street
but grandeur.' Or go to the street of *Lucre,* and enquire for
the house of the *Miser;* fie, there is no such person in it: or
for the house of the *murderer* amongst the physicians: or the
house of the *arrant thief* amongst the drovers, and see how
you would fare; you would sooner get into prison for enquiring, than get any body to confess his name. Yes, Hypocrisy
creeps between man and his own heart, and conceals every
iniquity so craftily, under the name and similitude of some
virtue, that she has made every body almost unable to recognise himself. *Avarice* she will call *economy.* In her language
dissipation is *innocent diversion; pride* is *gentility; a perverse*

man is a *fine manly fellow; drunkenness* is *good fellowship,* and *adultery* is only the *heat of youth.* On the other hand, if *she* and her disciples are to be believed, the *devout man* is only a *hypocrite* or a *blockhead;* the *gentle* but a *sneaking dog;* the *sober* a mere *hunks,* and so on. Send her, therefore," he continued, "thither, in her full array, I will warrant that she will deceive every body, and that she will blind the counsellors and the warriors, and all the officers, secular and ecclesiastical, and will draw them hither in multitudes presently, by means of her *mask of changeable hue."* And thereupon he sat down.

Then Beelzebub arose, the devil of *Inconsiderateness,* and with a rough, bellowing voice,—" I am," said he, "the mighty prince of *Bewilderment;* to me it pertains to prevent man from reflecting upon and considering his condition. I am the principal of those wicked, infernal *flies* which craze mankind, by keeping them ever in a kind of continual buz, about their possessions or their pleasures, without ever leaving them with my consent, a moment's respite, to think about their courses or their end. It ill becomes one of you, to attempt to put himself on an equality with me, for feats useful to the kingdom of Darkness. For what is Tobacco but one of my meanest instruments, to carry bewilderment into the brain? And what is the kingdom of *Mammon,* but a branch of my vast domain? Yea, if I were to recite the ties which I have on the subjects of *Mammon* and *Pride*—yea, and on the subjects of *Asmodeus, Belphegor,* and *Hypocrisy*—no man would tarry a minute longer under the rule of one of them. Therefore," said he, "I am the one to do the work, and let none of you boast again about his merits." Then Lucifer the Great arose himself from his burning throne, and with a would-be complaisant, but nevertheless frightful look on both sides,—" Ye master-spirits of eternal Night! ye supreme possessors of the cunning of Despair!" he said, "though the vast black gulf and the wilds of Destruction, are indebted to no one for inhabitants, more than to my own royal majesty, since I of yore, failing to drag the Omnipotent from his possession, drew millions of you, my swarthy angels, to this place of horrors, and have since drawn millions of men to you; nevertheless, it cannot be denied, that ye too have all done your part, to sustain this vast infernal empire."

Then Lucifer began to answer them one by one. "For one of late origin, I will not deny, O *Cerberus*, that thou hast brought to us many a booty from the island of our enemies, by means of tobacco, a weed the cause of much deceit; for how much deceit is practiced in carrying it about, in mixing it, and in weighing it: a weed which entices some people to bib ale; others to curse, swear, and to flatter in order to obtain it, and others to tell lies in denying that they use it: a weed productive of maladies in various bodies, the excess of which is injurious to every man's body, without speaking of his *soul:* a weed, moreover, by which we get multitudes of the poor, whom we should never get, did they not set their love on tobacco, and allow it to master them, and pull the bread from the mouths of their children.

"And as for you, my brother *Mammon*, your power is so universal, and likewise so manifest upon the earth, that it has become a proverb that '*any thing can be got for money.*' And undoubtedly," said he, turning to Apollyon, "my beloved daughter *Pride* is of great utility to us; for what is more capable of injuring a man in his condition, his body, and his soul, than that *proud, haughty idea*, which will make him squander a *hundred pounds* for display, rather than stoop to give a *crown* for peace. *She* keeps people so stiff-necked, with their sight so intent on lofty things, that it is a pleasure to see them, by staring and reaching into the air, falling plump into the abysses of Hell. As for you, *Asmodeus*, we all remember your great services of yore; no one keeps his prisoners more firmly under the lock, and no one meets with less rebuke than yourself—the whole rebuke, indeed, consisting in a little laughing, at what is called wanton tricks. Yes, Asmodeus, I admit that your power is very great; though I cannot help reminding you," he added, with a jocular though truly infernal grin, "that you were all but starved, above there, during the last dear years. As for you, my son *Belphegor*, lousy prince of Sloth, nobody has afforded us more pleasure than yourself, so very great is your authority amongst gentle and simple, even down to the beggar. Nevertheless, if it were not for the skill of my daughter *Hypocrisy*, in coloring and disguising, who would ever swallow one of your hooks? And after all, if it were not for the diligent firmness of my brother *Beelzebub*, in keeping men in *inconsiderate bewilderment*, I question whether all of you united would be worth a straw. Now," said he, "let us review the whole.

"What would you be worth, Cerberus, with your excessive sucking, if it were not for the assistance of Mammon? What merchant would ever fetch your leaves from India, through so many perils, if it were not for the sake of Mammon? And if it were not for *his* sake, what king would receive it, in Britain especially? And who, but for the sake of Mammon, would carry it to every corner of the kingdom? But, notwithstanding this, what wouldst thou be worth, Mammon, without Pride to squander thee upon fine houses, magnificent garments, needless litigations, music, horses and costly appurtenances, various dishes, beer and ale in a flood, far above the *means* and *rank* of the possessor; for if money were used within the limits of *necessity* and *propriety*, of what advantage would Mammon be to us? Thus you would be worth nothing without *Pride*; and little would *Pride* be worth without *Wantonness*, because bastards are the most numerous and the fiercest subjects, which my daughter *Pride* possesses in the world.

"You too, Asmodeus, prince of *Wantonness*, what would you be worth, if it were not for *Sloth and Idleness*; where but for them would you get a night's lodging? You could hardly expect it from a labourer or toiling student. And you, Belphegor of Idleness, who would welcome you a minute, attended as you would be with shame and reproach, if it were not for Hypocrisy, who conceals your ugliness under the name of *internal sickness*, or of a *well meaning person*, or under the shape of *despising riches* and the like.

"And she too, my dear daughter *Hypocrisy*, what is she worth, or what would she ever be worth, skilful and resolute sempstress as she is, if it were not for your help, my eldest brother *Beelzebub*, mighty prince of *Inconsiderateness*. If he would leave people leisure and respite, to seriously consider the nature of things and their difference, how often would they spy holes in the folds of the gold-cloth robe of *Hypocrisy*, and perceive the hooks through the bait? What man, did not Inconsiderateness deprive him of his senses, would chase baubles and pleasures—evanescent, surfeiting, foolish and disgraceful—and prefer them to *peace of conscience*, and glorious *everlasting happiness?* And who would hesitate to suffer martyrdom for his faith, for an hour or a day, or to endure affliction for forty or sixty years, if he would reflect that his neighbours here are suffering in an hour, more than he can ever suffer upon the earth?

"*Tobacco* then is nothing without *money*, nor money without *Pride*; and Pride is but feeble without Wantonness, and Wantonness is nothing without *Idleness*; Idleness without *Hypocrisy*, and Hypocrisy without *Inconsiderateness*. But," said Lucifer, (and he raised his fiendish hoofs on the fore claws,) "to speak my own opinion, however excellent all these may be, I have a *friend* to send against the she enemy of Britain, better than the whole."

Then I could see all the chief devils, with their ghastly mouths opened towards Lucifer, in anxious expectation of learning what this friend might be, whilst I was as impatient to hear as they. "The one I allude to," said Lucifer, "is called *Ease*; she is one whose merits I have too long disregarded, and whose merit, Satan, you yourself disregarded of yore, when in tempting Job you turned the unpleasant side of life towards him. She is my darling, and her I now constitute deputy, immediately next to myself, in all matters relating to my earthly government: Ease is her name, and *she* has damned more men than all ye together, and very few would ye catch without *her*. For in *war, or danger, or hunger, or sickness*, who would value *tobacco, or money*, or the pomposity of Pride, or would entertain a thought of welcoming either *Wantonness or Sloth*? Or who in such straits, would permit themselves to be distracted either by *Hypocrisy or Inconsiderateness?* No, no! they are too awake then, and not one of the infernal *flies of Bewilderment*, which shows its beak, will buzz during one of these storms. But *Ease*, smooth Ease, is the nurse of you all: in her calm shadow, and in her teeming bosom ye are all bred, and also every other infernal worm of the conscience, which will come to gnaw its possessor *here* for ever, without intermission.

"As long as *Ease* lasts, there is no talk but of some species of diversion, of banquets, bargains, pedigrees, stories, news, and the like. There is no mention of *God*, except in idle swearing and cursing; whereas the *poor* and the *sick*, who know nothing of ease, have God in their mouths and their hearts every minute.

" But go ye also in the rear of her, and keep every body in his sleep and his rest, in prosperity and comfort, abundance and carelessness; and then you will see the poor honest man, as soon as he shall drink of the alluring cup of Ease, become a perverse, proud, untractable churl—the industrious labourer change into a careless, waggish rattler—and every other person become just what you would desire him. Because pleasant *Ease* is what every one seeks and loves; she hears not counsel, fears not punishment—if good, she will not recognise it—if bad, she will foster it of her own accord. *She* is the prime-temptation; the man who is proof against *her* tender charms, ye may fling your caps to—for we must bid farewell for ever to his company. *Ease*, then, is my terrestrial *deputy*, follow her to Britain, and be as obedient to her as to our own royal majesty."

At this moment the huge bolt was shaken, and Lucifer and his chief counsellors were struck to the vortex of *extremest Hell*; and oh, how horrible it was to see the throat of Unknown opening to receive them! "Well," said the angel, "we will now return; but you have not yet seen any thing in comparison with the *whole*, which is within the bounds of *Destruction*, and if you had seen the whole, it is nothing to the inexpressible misery which exists in *Unknown*, for it is

not possible to form an idea of the World in extremest Hell."
And at that word the celestial messenger snatched me up to
the firmament of the accursed kingdom of Darkness, by a
way I had not seen, whence I obtained, from the palace along
all the firmament of the black and hot *Destruction*, and the
whole *land of Forgetfulness*, even to the walls of the *city of
Destruction*, a full view of the accursed monster of a *giantess*,
whose feet I had seen before—I do not possess words to
describe her figure. But I can tell you that she was a *triple-
faced giantess*, having one very atrocious countenance turned
towards the heavens, barking, snorting and vomiting accursed
abomination against the celestial king; another countenance
very fair towards the *earth*, to entice men to tarry in her
shadow; and another, the most frightful countenance of all,
turned towards *Hell*, to torment it to all eternity. She is
larger than the entire earth, and is yet daily increasing, and a
hundred times more frightful than the whole of Hell. She
caused Hell to be made, and it is she who fills it with
inhabitants. If *she* were removed from Hell, Hell would
become Paradise; and if she were removed from the earth,
the little world would become Heaven; and if she were to go
to Heaven, she would change the regions of bliss into utter
Hell. There is nothing in all the universe, (except herself,)
that God did not create. She is the mother of the four female
deceivers of the city of Destruction; she is the mother of
Death; she is the mother of every *evil* and *misery*; and she
has a fearful hold on every living man—her name is SIN.
"*He who escapes from her hook, for ever blessed is he!*" said
the angel. Thereupon he departed. and I could hear his
voice saying, "*write down what thou hast seen, and he who
shall read it carefully shall never have reason to repent.*"

The Heavy Heart.

Heavy's the heart with wandering below,
And with seeing the things in the country of woe;
Seeing lost men and the fiendish race,
In their very horrible prison place;
Seeing that the end of the crooked track
    Is a flaming lake,
    Where dragon and snake
    With rage are swelling.
I'd not, o'er a thousand worlds to reign,
    Behold again,
    Though safe from pain,
    The infernal dwelling.

Heavy's my heart, whilst so vividly
The place is yet in my memory;
To see so many, to me well known,

Thither unwittingly sinking down
To-day a hell-dog is yesterday's man.
      And he has no plan,
      But others to trepan
      To Hell's dismal revels.
When he reach'd the pit he a fiend became.
      In face and in frame.
      And in mind the same
      As the very devils.

Heavy's the heart with viewing the bed.
Where sin has the meed it has merited:
What frightful taunts from forked tongue.
On gentle and simple there are flung.
The ghastliness of the damned things to state.
      Or the pains to relate
      Which will ne'er abate
      But increase for ever,
No power have I, nor others I wot:
      Words cannot be got;
      The shapes and the spot
      Can be pictured never.

Heavy's the heart, as none will deny,
At losing one's friend or the maid of one's eye.
At losing one's freedom, one's land or wealth;
At losing one's fame, or alas! one's health;
At losing leisure; at losing ease;
      At losing peace
      And all things that please
      The heaven under.

At losing memory, beauty and grace,
    Heart-heaviness
    For a little space
    Can cause no wonder.

Heavy's the heart of man when first
He awakes from his worldly dream accursed,
Fain would be freed from his awful load
Of sin, and be reconciled with his God;
When he feels for pleasures and luxuries
    Disgust arise,
    From the agonies
    Of the ferment unruly,
Through which he becomes regenerate,
    Of Christ the mate,
    From his sinful state
    Springing blithe and holy.

Heavy's the heart of the best of mankind,
Upon the bed of death reclined;
In mind and body ill at ease,
Betwixt remorse and the disease,
Vext by sharp pangs and dreading more.
    O mortal poor!
    O dreadful hour!
    Horrors surround him!
To the end of the vain world he has won;
    And dark and dun
    The eternal one
    Beholds beyond him.

Heavy's the heart, the pressure below,
Of all the griefs I have mentioned now;
But were they together all met in a mass,
There's one grief still would all surpass;
Hope frees from each woe, while we this side
     Of the wall abide—
     At every tide
     'Tis an outlet cranny.

But there's a grief beyond the bier;
     Hope will ne'er
     Its victims cheer,
     That cheers so many.

Heavy's the heart therewith that's fraught:
How heavy is mine at merely the thought!
Our worldly woes, however hard,
Are trifles when with that compared:
That woe—which is known not here—that woe
     The lost ones know,
     And undergo
     In the nether regions:
How wretched the man who exil'd to Hell,
     In Hell must dwell,
     And curse and yell
     With the Hellish legions!

At nought, that may ever betide thee, fret
If at Hell thou art not arrived yet:
But thither, I rede thee, in mind repair
Full oft, and observantly wander there;
Musing intense, after reading me,

Of the flaming sea,
Will speedily thee
Convert by appalling.
Frequent remembrance of the black deep
Thy soul will keep,
Thou erring sheep,
From thither falling

JAMES M. DENEW, PRINTER, 72, HALL PLAIN, GREAT YARMOUTH.